Awaken: Sleeping Beauty Retold

DEMELZA CARLTON

Book 6 in the Romance a Medieval Fairy Tale series

Copyright © 2017 Demelza Carlton

Lost Plot Press

ISBN-13: 978-0-9922693-9-5

ISBN-10: 0-9922693-9-3

DEDICATION

For every one who's ever envied Sleeping Beauty a
good night's sleep.
New parents, insomniacs, and all the awesome readers
who can't put the book down until they know if it ends
in happily-ever-after. Because skipping to the end
would be cheating, right?

One

In King Erik's crowded cathedral, where countless courtiers jostled each other for a glimpse of their radiant new queen, Lady Margareta of Beacon Isle, Princess Rosamond stood alone.

Or as alone as a girl could be with some lady's elbow in her midsection and yet another baron's cape trying to sweep her veil from her head for the dozenth time that day. Rosamond wished she could have worn her hair uncovered, like Queen Margareta did, restrained only by a crown of roses.

Rosamond longed to be back outside in her own

garden at home, far from this foreign kingdom, but her father, King Almos, insisted that a girl her age was old enough to be betrothed, so here she was, an unwilling guest at someone else's wedding, while she wore the gowns and veils her mother had insisted upon in order to tempt some royal younger son to ask for Rosamond's hand in marriage.

Contrary to her father's wishes, Rosamond intended to keep her hands to herself for some time yet. If she could only...

The herald bellowed something about presenting their respects to the new king and queen. Rosamond found herself swept along in a wave of silk-clad humanity as the courtiers hurried to kiss the king's arse. Well, officially his hand, but if he'd turned around and presented his backside, they wouldn't have hesitated.

After what felt like forever, finally the herald announced, "Her Royal Highness, Crown Princess Rosamond, daughter and heir of King Almos..."

Rosamond didn't wait for him to finish listing her father's various titles. Instead, she strode forward and bobbed a curtsey to the king and queen as two guardsmen brought forward her coronation gift for the couple – a pair of pink rosebushes that matched the shade of Rosamond's dress perfectly.

Behind her, she heard the hiss of malicious

whispers from men who'd bowed so low their hats fell off and ladies who might as well have dropped to their knees when they'd curtsied. Rosamond lifted her head high, trying to ignore them.

To her surprise, both King Erik and Queen Margareta rose to offer Rosamond similar courtesies. As the queen straightened, she held out her hand to Rosamond, asking the girl to sit beside her.

Anything to get her out of the crush of bodies. Rosamond took the chair beside the queen happily.

"Where did you manage to grow such a delicate shade of pink?" Queen Margareta asked her. "I had an extensive rose garden in the house where I grew up, but all our roses were white." She paused to nod in acknowledgement to some courtier and his family who prostrated themselves face-down before the throne.

Rosamond tried not to laugh. "I am gifted with plants," she replied with no small amount of pride. "When I was born, my fairy godmothers blessed me with two talents – that of healing, and an affinity with plants. When my father heard of your wedding and coronation, he insisted that I bring you two of my finest roses as gifts. So here I am, and so are they."

"But how do you make them that colour pink?" Margareta asked.

"I asked them to make flowers the colour of my newest gown, so that I might wear them in my hair,"

Rosamond admitted. Her father's kingdom was not as rich as that of King Erik, which was richer still with the addition of Margareta's dowry of Beacon Isle, so Rosamond had fewer jewels than most of the courtiers present that day.

"So you are saying it is magic? That you can speak to plants, and they do your bidding?" Margareta said, looking intrigued. She removed her flower crown. "Here. Can you make these pink to match your gown, too?"

Rosamond took the wreath in her hands. The roses were wilting in the hot hall, poor things.

She had never tried to change the colour of cut roses, only those still attached to the bush, but she could not refuse the queen's request without at least attempting to fulfil it. Rosamond concentrated on the flowers, feeling the drying sap flow sluggishly through the stems as they valiantly tried to survive just a little longer.

There was no plant to talk to in the dying circlet. Sighing, Rosamond pricked her thumb on a thorn and sent a wave of healing into the twined flowers. The limp stems she touched stiffened once more, as waterfalls of wilting petals turned into perfect double crowns. Within moments, the queen's coronet looked as fresh as if had just been picked from the bush, ready formed, but they were no pinker than before. These

4

were as white as the moon.

"Oh, you have made them so beautiful!" Queen Margareta exclaimed in delight. "But I would so love them to be pink."

Swaying in her seat, Rosamond concentrated harder on the flowers. Now they were healed, they should do her bidding. They should...blush, just as the queen commanded. Blush as prettily as a maid surprised as she bathed. So they would be pink as...as...

Rosamond fainted before she could finish that thought.

Two

"Mistress, you must wake and eat something," Rosamond's maid urged.

Rosamond's head hurt, as it always did after she'd tried to perform magic. What sort of witch swooned whenever she cast a spell? One who shouldn't perform magic at all, her mother's voice echoed in her head. A princess, and a future queen, should be practicing protocol and learning all the arts of a highborn lady so that she could be an example to her subjects.

As this apparently didn't include spending long hours in the castle gardens, Rosamond had ignored her mother as much as possible. What was the point of being a queen if you couldn't do what you liked once in a while? After all, it was the king who ruled. Queens were just...for decoration, and doing whatever it was women did to get children. Oh, she knew it involved men and clothing was not required, but no one had been willing to tell her all the details. Her mother had promised to tell her everything on the night before her wedding.

Wedding. Ugh. Rosamond didn't fancy a single one of the noblemen she'd met at King Erik's court, and she fervently hoped the feeling was mutual. She'd be happy in her ignorance until the right man came to his senses and asked for her hand.

Just thinking about men made her head hurt all the more.

"Bring me willow bark tea first," Rosamond ordered.

"I have it here already, mistress," the maid said, sounding aggrieved.

"Give it to me, then."

A cup touched Rosamond's lips and she gulped down the contents, barely tasting the tepid tea.

"Now you must eat something," the maid insisted.

Rosamond gritted her teeth. Monika had been her maid for as long as she could remember, and she swore the girl liked to boss her around as much as

Rosamond's mother did. More, perhaps, because Monika was not much older than her mistress and Rosamond was certain she reported everything she said to Queen Maria, Rosamond's mother. Hence why Rosamond was stuck wearing the gowns and veils her mother had insisted upon for every royal event at court.

So Rosamond took the small loaf of bread Monika held out, broke off a piece and popped it into her mouth. Food helped combat the weakness she felt after casting a spell. More helpful was a visit to the palace gardens, where the plants would restore her far faster, but the memory of yesterday's whispering courtiers was enough to make her wish to keep to her chambers until she was well enough to return home. Under no circumstances did she want even one of them to see her in the palace gardens, talking to the plants. It only took one to spread vicious rumours.

But one vicious rumour might mean no marriage proposals, too, which would be a godsend in Rosamond's eyes. And she would so love to see the roses which had provided the queen's crown.

Rosamond stuffed the rest of the bread into her mouth, forgetting all propriety in her haste. With an effort, she swallowed. "Help me dress," she commanded.

Monika set her hands on her hips. "Are you sure

you're well enough? You've been abed, senseless, for a day and two nights, mistress."

The way Monika said it, she made "mistress" sound like "helpless child". This wasn't new.

Rosamond smiled sweetly. "I've rested plenty. Time to be up and about. Doesn't Mother want me to bring a husband home?"

Monika gave her a dark look, but all she said was, "If you hurry, we might make it to the tournament before it starts."

A tournament? Rosamond had heard of such things, but never attended one before.

"With knights? And jousting?" Rosamond asked eagerly.

"That was yesterday," Monika said, helping Rosamond change into a fresh shift. She selected a gown the colour of ripe strawberries and held it out for Rosamond to put on. "Today is the melee."

Rosamond slipped her arms through the sleeves and forced herself to stand still so Monika could thread and tie the laces of her gown. "What is a melee?"

"I am not sure," Monika admitted, giving the laces a sharp tug so that Rosamond was left breathless. "But Sir Warin has entered."

"Sir Warin? But who will guard me?" Rosamond demanded.

"You have a place beside the queen, if you are well enough," said Monika. "I'm sure her royal guard won't mind taking care of one more."

That sounded all right to Rosamond, so she submitted to Monika's toilette with good grace as the maid dressed her hair and tucked it under a white veil.

They made their way out to a field Rosamond barely recognised. Gone were the sheep that had grazed there when they'd arrived. Now it was crowded with brightly coloured pavilions crowned with flags that snapped in the breeze. At one end, there was tiered seating that held a crowd of courtiers. Rosamond suppressed a groan as she felt their eyes turn on her.

"This way, mistress," Monika said, touching Rosamond's elbow. She pointed at a stand shrouded in a purple canopy. In the shadows beneath it, Rosamond could just make out the king and queen.

Rosamond took her seat beside Queen Margareta and tried to hide her surprise as Monika placed herself on the boards at Rosamond's feet.

Margareta turned to Rosamond. "It is good to see you better, Princess."

Before Rosamond could reply, the king added, "She looks like a strawberry with cream on top. She'll distract the knights from combat in those colours. Ha, they'll all want to eat her up!" He laughed at his own joke, as did most of the courtiers within earshot.

Rosamond blushed as red as her dress.

"Do shut up, Erik, or the girl will return home convinced there's an ass on the throne here and her father's army will be at our gates within the week," Margareta said in a low voice, so that only Rosamond and the king heard. The queen's serene smile never faltered. "Now, Princess, let me look at you. He is right about one thing. That colour does suit you. I hope you brought a lot of favours, for all the knights will be asking for yours today."

"Favours?" Rosamond faltered.

Monika pushed a bundle of cloth into her lap with a pointed look.

"Is this your first tournament, Princess?" the queen asked. When Rosamond nodded, Margareta continued, "It is mine, too, but I have had both my husband and many of his knights explaining the intricacies of tournaments to me for weeks until I agreed that all of the men would be allowed to show off in my honour. Apparently, beating each other senseless is a sign of respect to their new queen. Quite barbaric."

While they waited for the day's combat to begin, Margareta regaled Rosamond with tales of yesterday's jousting. Two horses had been killed, several knights had broken arms and legs, and one was sporting two black eyes so dark he'd refused to remove his helmet.

Rosamond couldn't hide her shock. "You mean men were hurt? All I have heard of tournaments is that they are heroic. Romantic, for knights fight for their lady-loves. I had not heard that men were injured."

The king heard this and laughed. "Silly girl, of course men are hurt. This is good practice for battle. And just like in battle, we have physicians on hand to help set bones and the like."

Rosamond felt ill, as though she would bring her breakfast back up again at the king's feet.

"Erik," the queen said warningly.

The king opened his mouth as if to protest, then closed it again without a word and turned to face the empty field.

"I would like to hear more about how you choose your gowns, Princess," Margareta said. "First the pale pink at the coronation, and now this deeper rose for today. What will you choose tomorrow? Purple? So that on the day of your departure, you wear black?"

Embarrassed again, Rosamond mumbled something about how her mother had chosen her gowns for this trip.

"Then you are very lucky. My mother would be perfectly happy to send me out naked, as long as I wore a string of pearls," Margareta declared.

Rosamond couldn't help herself. She burst out laughing. "Your mother would let you go out naked?

Not even wearing a shift?"

Margareta nodded. "Naked. Clothing is just a distraction, she said, when the way to catch a husband is to show him what you will bring to the marriage. If you truly wish to enchant a man, let him see you naked. I assure you, it will torment him until he finds the courage to ask for your hand so that he can see such beauty again."

Rosamond doubted she would ever have the courage to do something so brazen. Not to mention that there was little chance she would ever want to enchant a man. King Erik seemed like a nice enough husband to Margareta, yet she'd called him an ass. If even the best men were donkeys, where did that leave her?

Thinking to change the subject, Rosamond ventured, "I can't imagine it. You look so lovely in your gown, Your Majesty. What manner of creature grows fur in such a rich red colour?"

The queen laughed. "This is not fur. It is velvet – made on a loom by a weaver who brought her knowledge of its craft from distant foreign lands. I shall make you a gift of some, if you wish it."

"I do," Rosamond said fervently.

Conversation ended for a little while, as a cacophony of trumpets signalled the beginning of the tournament. Two teams of knights lined up on opposite ends of a field, while a page in the king's colours set what looked like a blown-up pig's bladder in the middle of the field.

Rosamond turned to the queen to ask about the bladder, but someone blew a short blast on a trumpet and the thunderous clatter of two dozen men charging across a field toward one another drowned out any sound she made.

She lost sight of the bladder amid the madmen trying to kill each other, though only armed with wooden staves.

It was nothing short of brutal. She went from gasping at every blow to leaving her mouth permanently open. Rosamond tried to close her eyes but a fresh shout or crack of bone only made her snap her eyes open again until finally she clapped her hands over her eyes so she could only peek through her fingers. Even that limited field of vision made her sick to her stomach.

All around her, people cheered and groaned as their favourite knights gained or lost some sort of victory, but Rosamond couldn't tell one mud-spattered man from another, especially with them clad head to toe in boiled leather.

Finally, when she was certain she could endure no more of this violence, the king called a halt to the match. Servants stood beside the field with flagons and the squires raced to get their knights a drink. Only then did helmets come off, and Rosamond realised she recognised one of the half-dozen men left standing as the captain of her guard, Sir Warin.

The king saw him at the same time Rosamond did. "You man fights well," he said. "You should make sure he carries your favour into battle, for if he fights for one of the ladies in my court, I will do everything in my power to persuade him to stay in my service instead of your father's."

Her man. Rosamond hadn't thought of the knight that way before, but now that she looked at him, she had to admit he was quite handsome. He was no simpering courtier but a brave knight who fought well. Who would fight for the woman he loved, and her honour. She sighed. So romantic.

Rosamond flapped her hand to get Monika's attention. "Go to Sir Warin and give him this," she instructed, thrusting a piece of pink fabric at her maid. "Tell him he fights for his princess's honour."

Monika didn't say anything. She simply took the handkerchief and made her way from the royal stand to where Sir Warin stood, drinking his cup of ale.

The queen, noticing Rosamond's preoccupation, followed her gaze. "So that's why you aren't flirting with the courtiers here. You have better men at home."

Rosamond reddened. "I don't know how to flirt, Your Majesty. And even if I did…"

Margareta patted her hand. "Most men won't notice anyway. They're simple creatures, really. Let him kiss you, find a way for him to glimpse you naked, and then refuse all else until you are married. Everything else is just so you can make sure he's not a complete ass, right, Erik?"

"Mm?" the king said. His attention was on the remaining six men forming up on the field once more. "Yes, of course. They're about to fight again."

Margareta's serene smile surfaced as she added softly to Rosamond, "And never agree to host a tourney. I swear, this will be our last."

The horn blasted its command for the fight to begin, and Rosamond hid behind her hands. But if she peeped between her fingers, she could still see the pink handkerchief tied to the shoulder of Sir Warin's cuirass as six men became four, then three, then two, until he faced a single foe who was much larger than him.

Their staves clacked together like practice swords, but both men wielded them like steel blades they intended to kill one another with. They circled, crossed, thrust…it looked like an elegant dance, until Warin stumbled on an uneven patch of ground and his thrust went wide. His opponent saw his chance and brought his stave down hard against Warin's sword arm.

Rosamond heard the crack as Warin's arm broke, but the shouts and cheers from the stands drowned out her frantic cry.

The other man lifted his wooden sword in salute to the king, turning his back on Warin. Warin still held his stave in his injured arm, but he transferred it to his other hand and assumed a fighting stance.

"This is not over – I do not yield!" Sir Warin roared, loud enough for even Rosamond to hear.

Her heart beat rapidly in her breast. How could he be so brave, when he was injured?

The bigger man turned, and brought his stave up slowly. He, too, was tired, but he wasn't as badly hurt as Warin. The dance resumed. Warin's opponent dragged one foot, as though his knee had been damaged. Warin kept his broken arm close to his body, but as far away from the other man as possible. Each time the staves knocked together, it seemed softer, as though both men lacked the strength to continue.

Time ticked by. A second. An hour. An eternity. Or so it seemed to Rosamond, who longed to run out onto the field and heal her hero, but she could not until this duel was over.

A collective gasp rose from the stands as the big man overbalanced and fell to his knees. Warin, in an almost leisurely movement, set the point of his stave to the man's throat.

Rosamond heard wild cheering, and it took her a moment to realise the sound came from her own throat.

"Do we have a winner?" King Erik boomed.

Warin pulled the pink handkerchief from his cuirass and waved it above his head like a flag as he staggered to the royal box. When he reached it, he fell to his knees. "I am the victor, Your Majesties," he said.

"To the joy of your countrywomen. I'm sure they are glad they will be protected by an able knight like yourself for their journey home," the king replied.

Countrywomen? Oh, of course. Monika. Rosamond dismissed the maid from her mind easily. Sir Warin was the captain of the princess's guard. He would defend her with his life, before he even glanced at Monika.

That was why she needed to heal him. She might be a poor witch, but he had fought for her honour and won. Rosamond rose and descended to the grass, or what had been grass before the fighting had churned it into dust. Heedless of her gown or who saw, she knelt beside her valiant knight and reached for his broken arm.

Blood. She needed blood to cast a spell. There were no thorns today, so she scraped her hand along the edge of his stave until she felt the prick of a splinter. With her fingers bleeding, she touched her wounded knight, closed her eyes and concentrated on healing him.

She concentrated so hard she barely noticed when the spell sent her into yet another deep swoon.

Three

When Rosamond opened her eyes, she met the frightened gaze of a maidservant she did not know. The girl bobbed a curtsey, said, "I shall fetch the queen," and hurried off, leaving Rosamond alone.

Alone with a tray of food, at least, Rosamond noted, reaching for one of the strange orange berries. It burst like a bubble of white wine on her tongue. Eagerly, she reached for another.

"So you like cloudberries, too, Princess?" Margareta asked as she swept into the room. "Erik says they aren't sweet enough for his liking." She reached for one and popped it into her mouth. "More for me."

Suddenly awkward, Rosamond didn't know what to do. Surely she should curtsey, or offer the queen a chair. What did one do when a queen visited your bedchamber?

Margareta dragged a bench from the corner to the side of Rosamond's bed and enthroned herself on it. "Your maid tells me you are unwell, and must return home. The royal physician says you should not be moved, you are so gravely ill. What say you?"

Rosamond wet her lips. "I am fine, Your Majesty."

"Are you with child?" the queen demanded. "If he refuses to marry you, I can make the man change his mind." Her smile was fierce.

Rosamond shivered. "No, Your Majesty. I have not chosen a husband yet, and my father has not chosen one for me."

"Not with child, and not ill," the queen said, ticking them off on her long fingers. "Then whatever is the matter?"

"My…gift. The magic I was born with. It is not strong. When I try to use it, I…am not strong enough, either." Rosamond swallowed. "At home, I only used my powers on living plants, and it was not so bad. Here…on cut flowers, and on men, I am not strong enough."

Margareta laughed. "So, what you are saying is that

men are hard work while plants are not? I will agree with you there!"

Rosamond wasn't sure what to say to that. Queen Margareta was nothing like she'd expected. Fortunately, she was saved from finding a response by the entry of a maidservant carrying a wooden box.

"I have a gift for you," the queen announced, taking the box. "It has been a week since my coronation and…look!" She flipped open the lid and revealed the crown of roses she'd worn on her coronation day.

Yet…this could not be the same crown. The roses were as fresh as if they had just been picked, instead of dried out in the summer heat as they surely should have been.

"Whatever spell you cast on them, these roses will not die. They remain perfect. You are gifted with powerful magic, Princess. I have little magic, but I have placed a blessing on the crown. When you take a husband, he will be loyal to you from the day you first wear this crown until the day he dies. I would advise wearing it on your wedding day." Margareta set the crown back in its box, and closed the lid.

"Thank you," Rosamond said. She didn't have the heart to tell the queen that she didn't want any husband, loyal or otherwise. "I thought you said you would give me some of that new cloth to take home, not a crown."

"So I did!" the queen exclaimed. "I forgot to ask Penelope if she has enough, or whether she must make more for you. I will send someone directly."

The maidservant who'd brought the box was quickly despatched, but the queen stayed to tell Rosamond all about the remainder of the tournament, which she'd missed. From the sound of it, that was a good thing. The melee on foot had been followed by one where the combatants rode on horseback, and Margareta sounded almost gleeful at the number of broken limbs she described in vivid detail.

Rosamond's stomach roiled, making her regret breaking her fast at all.

Four

Three days Rosamond waited for the queen's gift, while watching the crowds at court dwindle as other guests returned to their homes. When Rosamond hinted at her plans to depart, too, Queen Margareta insisted that the princess's gift would be ready within the hour, but hours came and went with no sign of any cloth.

Finally, Rosamond lost patience and sent Monika to find the weaver. The maid returned with a puzzled look on her face.

"Did you say the weaver was a woman named

Penelope?" Monika asked.

Rosamond nodded. "That's what the queen called her. Yes."

"I found a Penelope. She is the queen's own dressmaker, not just a weaver, and a noblewoman in her own right. Lady Penelope is a knight's widow and the queen's companion. She has not been at court because her daughter is ill." Monika frowned. "She says that if you are willing to come to her chambers, she will measure you for a new gown directly."

"I do not understand. The queen said…" Rosamond stopped. She had been the queen's companion in place of Lady Penelope. Queen Margareta evidently did not wish to give her up until her original companion was at her side again. "No matter. I shall go now."

Monika led the way back to Lady Penelope's chambers, an airy apartment that was bigger than the one Rosamond had been given. Evidently the queen's companion was held in high regard.

"Her Royal Highness, Princess Rosamond," Monika announced.

Movement in the window alcove drew Rosamond's attention as a petite, dark-haired woman climbed down from the window seat, setting down her sewing. She bobbed a curtsey. "Your Highness. I'm Penelope. Queen Margareta told me you wanted a gown like her red velvet one, but when my daughter took ill, I could not leave her side." Penelope tilted her head to the side, like a curious bird. "I don't think the red would suit you. Too dark. Perhaps pink or sage..." She crossed the room and knelt by a chest beside a small couch that Rosamond realised was occupied.

The pale girl on the couch looked perhaps ten years old, but her skin had a waxen sheen like she was not long for this life. Rosamond's heart went out to the girl, and to her poor mother.

"Melitta fell ill so suddenly. For three days, she unpacked the chests of cloth that arrived in port last week, exclaiming over all the new colours. And on the fourth...she could not rise from her bed." Penelope's tears spilled over and she wept into her hands.

Melitta looked like she would never rise again, in Rosamond's opinion. Unless she could heal the girl. Rosamond glanced around the room, looking for something sharp. She spotted a strange contraption with a wheel mounted on a low table, and a short staff with a spindle sticking up from the table. Rosamond swiped her finger across the spindle, wincing at the sting as the sharp point drew blood, then knelt beside the girl.

Laying her hand on Melitta's forehead, Rosamond closed her eyes. She focussed first on cooling the girl's fever, then on ridding the girl's blood of the disease.

As Rosamond felt her own head grow fuzzy, she released the girl and rose unsteadily to her feet. She fumbled blindly for the windowsill, then cried out as something sharp pierced her hand. Yet something about the pain cleared her vision almost instantly.

Rosamond glanced down. She had grasped a briar rose growing through the window, and the thorns had bitten deep into her palm. In the back of her mind, somewhere in the memories of how her magical gifts were supposed to work, Rosamond remembered that her healing ability was linked to plants. Suppressing a second cry of pain, she wrapped her hand firmly around the flower stem, burying the thorns even more deeply, and reached for the girl with her free hand.

Within moments, the girl's eyes fluttered open. She coughed wetly before she murmured something that sounded like, "Mitera?" and coughed again.

"I am here," Lady Penelope said.

The disease had settled in Melitta's lungs. Rosamond felt blood trickle down her wrist, but she closed her eyes once more to focus on the girl's lungs, where fluid was making it hard for her to breathe. Rosamond concentrated, and the fluid seemed to lessen a little. Slowly at first, then more strongly, she poured what magic she had into the girl. Melitta coughed again, not so thickly this time, and Rosamond took hope as she rid the girl of the disease that had plagued her.

In triumph, Rosamond pushed away from the girl, panting, as black spots danced before her eyes. She would not swoon today, she swore. Today, weak as she was, she was mistress of her own magic.

Five

Rosamond surveyed the horses. They all looked well rested and well fed — perfect for the journey home. If anything, their loads were lighter, now that the king and queen had their coronation gifts.

"What is all this?" Warin demanded.

Half a dozen servants came into view, each pair bearing between them an enormous chest.

"From Queen Margareta and Lady Penelope." They set the chests down and took off back into the palace.

Lady Penelope? Oh, then this must be the cloth the queen promised her, Rosamond decided. She had not expected this much. Perhaps this was Lady Penelope's doing. After all, if it weren't for Rosamond, her daughter Melitta would be dead. Rosamond shivered. They were all but a breath away from death, though she hoped her life would hold a great many more breaths than just one.

"We are not taking those chests with us," Sir Warin said. His deep voice held a command that any of his guardsmen would hurry to obey.

Rosamond was no guardsman, though. The princess gave orders. She did not obey them. She smiled. "And refuse the queen's gift? I think not. That would be rude. Some might see it as a declaration of war."

Sir Warin snorted, but he did not say a word.

Monika stepped forward. "Mistress, the chests are too heavy for the horses to carry. But I could pack the cloth into the saddlebags on the packhorses. Then we need not refuse the queen's gift."

So Warin nodded curtly. "Do it, then." He strode away, muttering under his breath.

Rosamond admired each folded length of fabric as her maid packed them into the saddlebags. There was pink, as Penelope had promised, but also sage, gold, cream, and a deep red that her mother might fancy. The only colour missing was blue. As the queen seemed to favour blue gowns for her wardrobe,

Rosamond supposed that the queen had used all the blue fabric already and Lady Penelope had not had time to weave more. No matter. There was enough rich fabric here to keep her mother's dressmaker sewing into winter. Rosamond liked that idea. She could have new gowns for Yule.

Finally, they were finished. Sir Warin returned, with a squad of guards in tow. Princess Rosamond mounted her horse, and Monika did the same. They had said their farewells to the king and queen the previous evening, before retiring, so now they formed up and rode out the gate, with far less fanfare than when they had arrived.

Nevertheless, when Rosamond glanced back at the palace she saw the queen standing at the battlements, dressed in blue and waving a blue handkerchief in farewell.

Six

Rosamond tired easily on the first day, and the second, and the third. When the guards pitched her pavilion by the setting rays of the sun, she had been quite ready to retire early for the first week of their journey home. Perhaps travelling did not agree with her, or the magic she had expended in healing Lady Penelope's daughter Melitta had taken its toll on her strength. She might not have swooned, but she was certain if she tried to use her magic again, she would most certainly faint.

So she stumbled to bed with the sun, falling asleep to the low hum of conversation between the guards,

Monika and Sir Warin. Aside from Monika and Warin, the others maintained a respectful silence in her presence, but once she was inside the pavilion, they thought nothing of making bawdy jokes that still made her blush. So much for not knowing what a couple did on their wedding night, though that seemed tame compared to their stories about the goings-on in the brothels they'd visited while staying in King Erik's capital.

Usually, Monika rode at her side. No matter how many times she asked Sir Warin to ride with her, he insisted that he was better at protecting her than making conversation that would amuse her.

Rosamond privately disagreed. Monika said little, and what she did say usually involved minding the skirt of her gown, or not overexerting herself. It was like travelling with her mother.

At the end of the sixth day, Rosamond was delighted to find Sir Warin riding beside her. "Welcome home, Princess."

Rosamond glanced around, but she saw nothing new except the edge of a wood they were about to enter. "Are we home already?" she asked, wrinkling her nose in puzzlement.

"You are, for those bramble hedges mark the boundary of your kingdom, Princess. One of your ancestors decreed that his borders must be marked with berry bushes, and no one disobeyed the king, so it was done. Now the thickets are so dense the farmers at the borders regard them as another crop. If we didn't export our berry wine, every man in the kingdom would be drunk as a lord, every day of the year!" Sir Warin laughed.

Rosamond shuddered. She'd seen far too many drunk lords at King Erik's court. There were so many reasons she didn't want a husband.

Sir Warin had not been drunk, though. She had never seen him anything but sober and alert, as befit a knight and a captain of the guard.

Could a princess marry a knight? Her mother had told her to look for a prince or a lord at least, but they were all foreigners. A knight who was her own countryman was surely more acceptable than some foreign barbarian, no matter what title he held. Sure, foreigners might bring extra lands to the kingdom, but what need had they for more land? Her kingdom's borders were already marked by berry bushes. If they expanded their territory, her people would have to plant more bushes just to know where the boundaries lay.

Rosamond trailed her fingers through a bush that grew beside the road, and felt an overwhelming sense of welcome, as if the plants were as delighted as she was that she would soon be home again.

Rosamond almost laughed. Such sentimental nonsense. Plants didn't have feelings. She stripped off a handful of berries and nibbled on them as she rode.

Sir Warin called a halt, setting up camp in a clearing amid a collection of particularly bountiful berry bushes. Some of the guards had picked handfuls already, but Sir Warin called them to set up camp first. They set to work as Rosamond slid from her mount, intent on picking her own share of the red berries before her greedy guards could choose the best ones.

For when it came to picking wild berries, a princess had as much right to them as the lowliest peasant. Her several times great-grandfather, the first King Almos from whom her father got his name, had decreed as much when he ordered the berry bushes to be planted, and no one had dared to rescind his law. Why would they? There were berries aplenty. Far more than the royal household could ever need.

But the more she picked, the stronger the feeling of welcome became. Rosamond thrust both hands deep into a berry bush, heedless of the thorns, and grasped a branch thicker than her arm. Power surged into her – like magic, but more, somehow. It coursed through her, singing of leaves and buds and berries, sap flowing and new growth stretching toward the sky, with the thunderous percussion of the deep draught of sustenance roots drew from the rich soil. The bush lived, with as much passion as she did, and it bade her welcome home.

"Are you all right, mistress?" Monika called, making her way over.

Rosamond released the bush, and wiped the tears from her cheeks. Never would she have thought plants could have such powerful emotions, let alone share them with her. "I'm fine," she said.

"No, you're not. Look at your poor hands!"

Rosamond glanced at the slight scratches on her hands, which faded even as she watched. The blood that had trickled from the cuts still looked ominous, though. "I am fine," Rosamond repeated, lifting her chin as she looked Monika in the eye. Her maid did not look fine at all. In fact, she looked unusually pale, with a thin sheen of sweat on her face. "Are you well?"

"Of course, mistress," Monika said. "It is hot, is all. Perhaps I have been too close to the fire. Surely you are thirsty. Shall I fetch you a drink?"

Monika needed refreshment more than Rosamond, but the princess followed her maid back to the pavilion where there was a jug of cider waiting for her. For them both, Rosamond corrected, making sure the maid poured two cups instead of one.

She vowed to watch Monika carefully tonight. The woman was certainly behaving very oddly.

Seven

Rosamond lay in the darkness of her pavilion, listening to Monika's even breathing. Low voices outside told her that the guardsmen were still awake, sitting around the fire, she presumed. After falling asleep almost instantly for a week, she was restless.

Perhaps it was the magic of communicating with the berry bush today, or maybe it was simply because she knew she was home. Rosamond was not sure, but she certainly did not feel like sleeping.

The sound of Sir Warin's deep voice decided her. Her maid might sleep, but Rosamond was not ready to retire yet. She neatened her gown as best she could in the darkness, then pushed aside the tent flap to emerge into the firelight.

Silence greeted her.

Only Sir Warin dared to break it. "Good evening, Princess," he said. "Are we making too much noise, so that you cannot get your beauty sleep? Though a princess such as yourself has no need to be any more beautiful than she is already."

Rosamond felt a blush colour her cheeks. She prayed it was too dark for Sir Warin to see the effect of his compliment. "I could not sleep," she confessed. "I thought perhaps a cup of wine..."

"Ludd, fetch the princess some wine," Sir Warin said. One of the guardsmen rose to do his bidding.

By the time the guardsman returned, the rest of the men had melted into the darkness. Once Rosamond had accepted the cup Ludd offered, he disappeared, too.

"Where did they go?" she asked Sir Warin, who alone had remained.

He stirred the fire. "Not far," he said. "Like every other night on this journey, they form a perimeter to protect you, Princess. Some will sleep, while others stand watch. We may be home, but it does not do to relax one's guard. There are still dangers on the road."

"Dangers?" Rosamond swallowed. "Who would

dare attack a royal travelling party in our own kingdom?"

"Not who, but what. There are bears and wolves in these woods, and there are tales of evil witches in the world who respect no borders. It is my duty and theirs to protect you from all dangers until I return you home to the king and queen." Sir Warin bowed his head. "I will not let any harm come to you, Princess."

His words made her feel oddly warm inside, which had nothing to do with the wine or the fire, she was certain. As though he took his responsibility for her safety personally. She liked that. Rosamond drank deeply from her cup. "Would you lay down your life me?" she asked. She licked the wine from her lips.

"As the captain of your guard, it is my duty to do so. But it will not come to that." He laughed. "No one has seen a wicked witch in these parts for many a long year, and any one of my men is easily a match for a wolf or a bear."

"I have never seen a wolf, or a bear," she mused.

Sir Warin laughed again. "And I hope you never do, Princess. One day you will be queen, and you will live in your castle, ruling over all of us, and in return we will keep the castle safe from bears and wolves and even witches."

"How do you defeat a witch?" Rosamond asked. "I thought only a more powerful witch could defeat another. There are tales of enchantresses who..." She tried to dig out the memory, but her head was too fuzzy.

"I am but a common soldier," Warin said ruefully, touching his arm. "Good with a sword, and little else. That is why you healed my arm, was it not? So that I might wield a sword in your defence, as you practice your benevolent witchcraft for the benefit of the kingdom. You will be a powerful queen one day, Princess. It would be an honour to lay down my life for you."

Rosamond laughed softly. "You are so sweet to say that," she said. "No man has ever..."

He was so close. So close and warm and tempting and...

Rosamond kissed him. For a moment, everything was perfect as her lips connected with his. Then, the moment shattered as he stiffened and pulled away.

"Your pardon, Princess," he said. "I fear you have mistaken me for someone else."

Rosamond licked her lips. He tasted of wine and salt, and she rather liked it. "No, Sir Warin. I gave a brave knight a kiss, as I should have when you won the melee at the tournament."

He stared at her for a long moment, before muttering something about checking the perimeter. He disappeared into the darkness.

For a long time, Rosamond waited for him to return. When he did not, and her eyelids began to droop, she returned to her pavilion. There were seven more nights before they arrived home, and a week was more than she would need to convince the knight that she was the woman for him.

After all, her mother had ordered her to find a husband while she was away, and no one disobeyed the queen.

Smiling to herself, Rosamond drifted off into sleep.

Eight

When Rosamond awoke the next morning, she couldn't smell breakfast.

"Monika?" she murmured, but received no answer. Perhaps it was too early and the maid was still preparing it. Rising, Rosamond decided to begin making herself presentable for the day. There was still a jug of water half full from last night, so she used that to wash before hunting for a comb to untangle her night-mussed hair.

A terribly unladylike snore made her stop, for it came from Monika's pallet. Surely the maid had not allowed a guardsman to sleep in her mistress's pavilion? She would soon feel the rough edge of Rosamond's tongue if she had. Wait until the queen heard about it.

Rosamond marched over to Monika's bed and wrenched the coverlet aside. Monika herself lay there alone, breathing so laboriously that it sounded like snoring.

"Monika, wake up. I need breakfast," Rosamond ordered.

The maid slept on.

Angrily, Rosamond shook the woman, but Monika simply fell back to her pallet, as limp as one of the rag dolls Rosamond had once played with as a child. She seemed unusually warm to the touch, too.

Feeling fear for the first time, Rosamond cupped Monika's cheek so she could gaze upon her face. The maid's eyes were closed, but her skin had the same waxy sheen as Melitta.

Rosamond tore her hands away from Monika and stumbled out of the tent as fast as she could. "It's Monika! She won't wake. She won't wake!" she shouted.

Strong hands fastened around her shoulders, spinning her around to face Sir Warin. "What's this about Monika?" he asked, his eyes filled with concern.

"She didn't wake. She usually wakes before me. I

called her. I even shook her, but she won't wake!" Rosamond babbled, shaking her head. "She is ill. The same ailment as the weaver's daughter, I know it!"

Sir Warin gestured to the nearest guard. "Is anyone else ill?"

The man shook his head. "I don't think so, sir. I'll go check the other men." He returned a few minutes later, still shaking his head. "No, sir. Not a single man still abed, seeing as the sun is so high in the sky and all. If the princess had risen earlier, as is her usual habit, maybe one or two might have been but..." He coughed. "I'll go help saddle the horses, sir."

"Monika usually wakes me," Rosamond said. "I don't understand. If she is so ill, why am I not ailing? She rarely leaves my side."

Sir Warin's eyes narrowed. "What has she done that you have not since we left the city?"

Rosamond spread her arms wide. "Everything." Princesses did not do things for themselves, Monika and her mother had told her so many times it had become a habit. "She cooks for me, packs my things, brings water to wash with, sets out my clothes and helps me dress, even mends my clothes when I tear them. When we get home, she says I must have new gowns made with the queen's gifts, because my travel-stained dresses will not be fit for anything more than rags. Those new velvets will be perfect for court..."

She might have prattled on for longer, but Sir Warin held up a hand to silence her.

"You said the weaver's daughter was ill, and Monika has the same ailment?" he asked.

Rosamond nodded.

"Did you touch the cloth the queen gave you?"

Rosamond's mouth seemed suddenly too dry. "I…no. It came in so many chests, and you were angry, so Monika said…she said she would load them onto the packhorses. The weaver's daughter unpacked those chests when they arrived, at about the same time we did, but no one else had touched them…" She stopped dead, clapping her hand to her horrified mouth. "You don't think Queen Margareta gave us cursed cloth?"

"Mayhap the queen herself did not know. Whether she did or no, the curse is undoubtedly real. We cannot take it home." Warin pointed at four guardsmen. "You! Fetch more wood. We must have a bonfire before we leave this spot."

The men obeyed, piling wood beside the small morning cookfire. They coaxed the cheerful flames into a roaring blaze under Warin's watchful eye, until he nodded and strode off.

"Where are you going?" Rosamond demanded, following him.

"To the picket lines, where the packhorses' burdens

are piled, to fetch the cursed cloth. I will do what I must to protect you and the kingdom." He marched grimly to the pile of bags, seizing several before heading back to camp. When he reached the fire, he unfastened one of the sacks, reached inside, and tossed the bundle of cloth onto the flames.

"No!" Rosamond shouted. "You can't burn the queen's gifts. They are gifts. To do so would start a war." She seized the next bundle of cloth before Sir Warin could throw it into the fire. "You can't!"

Warin wrenched it out of her grip. "Do not touch the cursed stuff, Princess. What the queen does not see, she will never know. Unless you know how to remove curses, we must destroy it with fire. Can you break curses, Princess?"

Rosamond wrapped her arms around herself as tears sprang to her eyes. No one had ever spoken so roughly to her before. "No. I am a healer, and I help plants. Only a powerful enchantress – "

"Then let me do my job, Princess, which is protecting you." Another bundle of bright-coloured cloth landed in the fire, sending up a shower of sparks, followed by two more.

Realisation dawned. "If she was cursed by merely touching the cloth, then so are you." Rosamond gulped. "So am I."

"I pray that you are not, Princess." Warin would

not meet her eyes. He turned and cupped his hands to his mouth, shouting for the attention of his men. "Ride for the capital. Tell the king we were taken ill on the road. God willing, we will be but a day behind you." He gave Rosamond a hard look. "You should go with them, Princess. Monika and I are cursed, but you are surely free of such evil spells."

Rosamond's fingers itched where she'd touched the velvet. "No, I cannot. What if you are wrong, and it is not a curse, but some plague that others can catch from me? I dare not bring it home."

"Go with them, Princess," Warin said through gritted teeth. "They will keep you safe. When this illness takes hold, I know that I cannot."

She lifted her chin as she glared at him. "Who will keep them safe from me if you are wrong? I am a Princess and a healer, and they will be no help to me when they are dead." She swallowed. "Or if I am dead, for surely the disease will take me first." She closed her eyes in horror. She didn't want to die. She didn't want him to die. Or Monika. Or anyone.

"Can you heal it?" Warin demanded.

Rosamond thought of Melitta. "Yes, perhaps. But it may take some time. We can't stay here beside the road, where any traveller might happen upon us, lest they be afflicted, too. We will need shelter while I try to heal you."

"Heal all three of us," Warin corrected, surrendering the last piece of cloth to the flames. "First Monika, then yourself, and if you have the energy and I still live, you can heal me."

Rosamond did not know how to heal herself, but she didn't tell Sir Warin that. She drew herself up. "Find us shelter, and I shall."

He nodded. "There is an old convent near here that I know of. It is one of the best spots in the kingdom for hawking, but as the king and queen are not fond of falcons, we should be safe."

"What about the nuns?" Rosamond demanded, horrified. "Their faith will not save them from whatever disease we are carrying, or a curse."

Warin flashed a bleak smile. "The convent has stood empty for my lifetime, Princess, and that of my father. The order who built it left, and did not come back. At least if we die there, it will be on hallowed ground."

Rosamond did not want to die, but she saw no other choice. "Help me with Monika. We must get her to this convent you speak of so that I may heal her." Before it was too late, she thought but didn't say.

Nine

After travelling for most of the afternoon, Rosamond wanted to scream at Sir Warin for his mistaken idea of what nearby meant. Even when they stopped, she saw no sign of any building at all. Perhaps the knight had only imagined this convent.

"In here," he said, taking Monika in his arms. He carried the unconscious maid toward a rock covered in thick briars.

No, not a rock. A stone wall, Rosamond realised. The briars bore so many flowers that they hid the joins in the stonework. "How do we get in?" she blurted out.

"When I was a boy, there was an entrance here. Under the briars, it will be here still." Sir Warin glanced down at Monika. "I will set her down. Keep watch over her while I work." He placed Monika carefully on the grass, then unsheathed his sword.

"No!" Rosamond cried out. "You don't need to cut them. I will ask the plants to move." The instant the words left her lips, she regretted them. Yes, plants usually did her bidding, but these were not the small rose trees in her garden at home. No, these were mighty monsters, wild and free. Yet she swallowed and stepped up to the tangled briar. Cupping her hands around a full-blown pink rose, she felt the sting as the tiny, needle-sharp thorns at the base of the bloom pierced her skin. "Permit us to pass," she whispered, closing her eyes.

She felt an answering whisper of greeting as she heard the rustle of leaves, moving in the breeze and scraping against stone. Except...there was no breeze in this still hollow.

Rosamond's eyes flew open. Before her, the briars had parted to reveal an arched portal into the building. She expected it to lead into darkness, but the ruined roof was open to the sky, letting in dappled sunlight.

Sir Warin stared at her with an intensity that made her feel uncomfortable. "I am glad to be on your side,

Princess. I would hate to be your enemy," he said. He lifted Monika's limp form and strode into what remained of the convent.

Rosamond hesitated for a moment, before following him inside what turned out to be a chapel. Little remained except the stone altar, which was now wreathed in roses. She stepped up to the altar, brushing aside the leaf litter that had collected on its surface. "Put her here," she commanded.

Now it was Sir Warin's turn to hesitate. "Witchcraft in a holy chapel? Won't we be struck down?"

Rosamond made an impatient sound in her throat. "We are already struck down with a curse, remember? Perhaps the holiness will help. We will need all the help we can get, for I am but a novice at this."

Reluctantly, he set Monika on the altar. Then he backed away, staring at the maid in horror. "She looks like one already dead, laid out for burial," he whispered. "Save her, Princess. Please, I beg you. Save us all." He dropped to his knees.

Save them all. If only she could.

Rosamond wrapped her hand around a tangle of briar, feeling warm blood slick her palm, before she set her other hand on Monika's breast and sent her healing magic flowing through the dying maid.

Ten

Three days it took her to heal Monika of the disease, for Rosamond's waning strength took its toll on how much magic she could use before she swooned. Even calling on the roses for assistance did not help as much as she had hoped...for Rosamond knew the disease coursed through her blood, too, threatening to steal her life, even as Monika recovered.

Sir Warin had caught a plump bird, which now roasted over the fire he'd built in the old convent courtyard. "Good evening, Princess," he greeted her, wiping at the thin sheen of sweat that seemed to permanently coat his brow. He had caught the plague, too, Rosamond realised, but he would not allow her to heal him until Monika was well.

Which was now.

"It is a good evening," she replied. "The last of the disease is gone from her body. She sleeps now, but soon she will wake. Monika is healed."

He flashed a tired smile. "Then you are truly a good witch and a worker of miracles, Princess. I am grateful for your care, and I am certain that when she wakes, Monika will be, too."

"I must heal you," Rosamond insisted. "Monika will be weak for a while yet. She will need your help, and you cannot return to the city if you carry the sickness."

"She will have you, Princess. You have enough strength for a whole kingdom."

Rosamond wanted to laugh at the irony of his statement. She barely had the strength to stand. She knew what the knight did not – that she had contracted the disease when she healed Melitta, and soon she would no longer be able to hide it from him. She suspected she had only lasted so long because the healing energy coursing through her into Monika had kept the disease at bay somewhat. Not enough, though. It was only a matter of time before the disease won. Rosamond could not heal herself – magic didn't work that way.

If Sir Warin would not allow her to heal him, then she would wait until he was asleep tonight and take care of him then, Rosamond decided. She had so little time left.

Fortunately, she didn't have long to wait. Sir Warin had scarcely finished his dinner before he stretched out before the fire, mumbling something about the lateness of the hour.

Rosamond's eyes darted to the sky, where the sun had not yet set. Sir Warin was sicker than he was willing to admit, too.

He had chosen a patch of grass to lie on, so Rosamond lay beside him. One of the briars on the wall had sent runners snaking through the grass, which was all she needed to help her heal him. At least, she hoped it would be enough.

Grasping a handful of thorny runners, she sent a wave of healing through Sir Warin's sleeping body. She would not have days for this; if she did not heal him completely in one go, she might not manage to heal him at all. So even as her head ached and her body grew numb, still Rosamond worked her magic. The brave knight must survive, even if she did not.

The full moon had risen high in the sky by the time she had rid Sir Warin of his ailment. He would sleep for some time yet, as his body still had healing of its own to do. If she were stronger, she would help him, but as it was…

She climbed laboriously to her feet. Rosamond wanted to check Monika one more time before she lay down to await her fate. There would be no healer to save the princess, but Rosamond knew this was the only way to save the kingdom. She could not carry this curse home.

Rosamond had already chosen her resting place. She believed it had once been a kind of courtyard, open to the sun and rain, because very little of the roof had fallen onto the mosaic tiles still visible beneath the leaf litter. In the middle of it stood a fountain, though it held no water now. Instead, the basin had filled up with roses, so that it resembled a bed of flowers. This would be her deathbed. Far more befitting of a princess than the cold vaults beneath her parents' castle. A castle she would never see again.

Would her last sight on this earth be of sunny blue skies or sparkling stars? Rosamond wondered. It mattered little. She would be surrounded by the scent of roses, which would be enough.

With considerable effort, she made her way to the chapel where Monika lay resting.

Rosamond laid a hand on the maid's forehead, searching for signs of the disease, but finding none.

"Mistress?" Monika croaked.

"Rest. You were ill, but you are better now,"

Rosamond soothed her, struggling to keep her voice from shaking. No one would reassure her when the time came. "Sir Warin sleeps in the courtyard, but he will wake when he is well, too."

"What of you, mistress? Who cares for you?" Monika asked.

No one. Rosamond didn't dare speak the words aloud. "I am well cared for, I assure you. My sleeping chamber is over there. The roses guard me while I sleep. They will allow no harm to come to me." For she would soon be beyond harm, and the kingdom would be safe.

"Mistress..."

"It is time for me to retire. I only came to check on you. If Sir Warin survives until morning, you must return with him."

"What of you, mistress?" Monika said again, more urgently this time.

Rosamond smiled sadly. "If I do not succumb before morning, then I will return with you. If my body lacks the strength to fight this plague...you must leave me here. Do not bring my remains home. Tell my parents I died on the road, of an illness that I would not wish to visit upon my people. Promise me, Monika."

"No, mistress!" Monika tried to rise, but she was too weak.

"Thank you for your service to me. Please thank Sir Warin, too, when he wakes."

And with that, Rosamond bent her final steps toward the rose-shrouded fountain. Perhaps it was selfish to use the last of her strength to reach the pretty courtyard, but she did not care. She had used so much of what she had left to heal others. If she did not put enough distance between herself and her travelling companions, they might contract the disease again from her remains, and she would not be around to heal them a second time.

When she reached the stone basin, she nearly tumbled in, she was so tired. The briars would not let her, though, snaking beneath her to hold her weight until they formed a proper bed. Thorns shredded her clothes and some pierced her skin, but she felt little any more.

The world was no more than a dream to her now.

Rosamond lay on her bed of roses, weaving her fingers between the blossoms. She could feel the disease running riot through her blood, though it had not invaded her lungs as it had Melitta, Monika and Sir Warin. As her energy waned, she fancied she felt the tiny disease motes slowed their dance, almost as if they would die with her. That was a good thing.

The briars she touched – a dozen bushes, at least, all sending their runners toward her – offered her welcome, wishing her health in ways that felt like sap running through her veins instead of blood.

Protect me, she told them, envisioning vines closing off the courtyard to all but the sky, so that no one could reach her while the disease still survived in her body. Protect the kingdom. In her mind's eye, this involved all the plants in the kingdom forming up like armies for battle, keeping anyone at bay who might threaten her people with a plague like hers.

She lay facing the sky, but Rosamond saw neither stars nor moon as her eyes closed and her consciousness sank into oblivion, surrounded by the plants she loved, promising to obey her wishes.

While she lay alone in the moonlight, briars wove themselves into an impenetrable wall, blocking off the courtyard. Leaves whispered in the night breeze, telling trees and bushes of the princess's desire, until every bush along the borders had heard her final command.

Roses cradled her body, while berry bushes built a wall of their own around her lands. They would keep the kingdom safe for her, they promised, as only plants can.

Eleven

"You should be here, planning a coronation ceremony and ruling the kingdom. Not riding about, chasing birds in the woods!" Lady Schutz hissed.

Lord Siward sighed. "Grandmother, this kingdom is so small, it almost rules itself. And it has been scarcely three weeks since the king died. The earth has not even had time to settle over his grave. It would be an insult to his memory to attempt to steal his throne before we know whether an heir can be found."

"Normal kingdoms name a new king on the same day the old one dies. A kingdom should not be without a ruler for even a day!" she insisted.

"If only our kingdom could be normal, but it is not. Neither is it without a ruler. I am not leaving the kingdom. I am simply riding out of the city for a little while. I shall visit the borders and the outlying villages, make sure all is well, and if I choose to spend a day or two hawking, what of it? It is the sport of kings, after all, and you are so set on me becoming one. It seems to me I should enjoy some of the privileges, seeing as I already shoulder the burdens of a position which are not mine to bear."

She threw her wrinkled hands up into the air. "Be it on your own head, then, if some other noble tries to claim the throne while you are playing with birds!"

"If some madman attempts it, then he is welcome to the throne," Lord Siward snapped. If only another man would lay claim to that much-vaunted chair, then he could do the job his father had done, instead of trying to rule in the king's stead. If they could find an heir...

But there was no heir. The king and queen had managed to have one child, and she had died young. A normal kingdom could ask for a near relation who had married into one of the royal families of a neighbouring kingdom, but this was no normal kingdom.

So that left him. Siward sighed, knowing he would

have to ascend the throne on his return. No other man in court was capable of ruling, though others had blood far more noble than his. Yet the king on his deathbed had appointed him Regent, for his sins.

All the more reason to take this trip now, for it might be his last chance at freedom before the heavy yoke of kingship settled on his shoulders.

His head started to clear as he left the city. Perhaps it was the lack of courtly arse-kissing, or maybe it was the clean scent from the woods instead of the smoke from cookfires, but he took heart when the city walls vanished from sight.

It was easily a week's ride to the border by way of the main road, but checking the borders was his first task. Every year, like his father and grandfather before him, Siward rode the borders, checking for signs of weakness. He hadn't found one yet, but if ever there was a time he needed one…it was now.

When he arrived at the end of the road, Siward sighed. He hadn't expected any change, though he had hoped for one.

Bramble hedges soared into the sky, forming a wall more formidable than simple stone. This wall ringed the kingdom, allowing no one in or out, and it had stood since his grandfather's time. His grandfather, Lord Schutz, had said the Wall had been a simple hedge once, but when the princess passed, the plants had risen up in protest to protect the kingdom. Siward never understood what they protected the kingdom from, for his grandfather had rambled considerably in his old age. Sometimes, he'd said it was to prevent a plague. At other times, he'd insisted it was to prevent war with a neighbouring kingdom, who had apparently killed the princess.

The truth of the tale was lost in time – and with his grandfather, who had lain in his grave for many years now.

Yet the Wall still stood, testament to some mysterious truth. Perhaps someone had cursed the kingdom, Siward decided. It seemed as good an explanation as any. If it weren't for the Wall, he could send messengers to neighbouring kingdoms to search for an heir. With it...he would be king.

The first time he'd seen the Wall, Siward had slashed at it with his sword, determined like a hundred other men before him that he could cut his way through. The brambles would have none of it, wrapping tendrils around his sword until they dragged it from his hand as they repaired the damage to the Wall as though he had never sliced a single stroke. The Wall was magic, most certainly. Which made it all the harder for a soldier like himself to understand. There were no witches in the kingdom, so whoever had cast it must be on the other side of the Wall, and out of his reach.

Astor, his hunting hawk, ruffled her feathers as if impatient to do something more than sit on her perch.

"You have the right of it, my friend," Siward told the bird, pulling off the creature's hood. "Let us hunt, and forget politics for a time. Worrying about it will not bring down the Wall."

He headed off the road, toward a spot known only to his family. It had the best hawking in the kingdom, and so it would continue as long as its location remained a closely-kept secret. Not even his grandmother knew this spot, he'd wager, for she had no desire to hunt.

He unhooded Astor, held his fist high in the air, and watched the bird fly off with powerful wingbeats. Siward wished for a moment that he could fly with her, high above the Wall, to see the world outside. Was it so different to their kingdom? As long as the Wall stood, he would never know.

With his eyes on Astor, Siward urged his horse to follow the bird. The forest was not so dense here, though there was no village nearby. Perhaps there once had been one, but it had been too close to the border that before the Wall it had been attacked too many times until it had been abandoned. Surely there would have been some ruins left, then, to mark where the town had stood. Yet Siward had never seen them.

Perhaps the brambles and briars had consumed those, too.

Astor hovered, and Siward held his breath for a moment before the hawk dived, gracefully seizing a bird on the wing before her prey had even been aware of her presence. Astor swooped down with her catch still in her talons, toward a briar-shrouded rock.

Siward thought she would perch on the rock, but Astor dipped down behind it and disappeared. Swearing, he rode around, trying to find the bird, but the rock seemed solid on all sides, and the bird was nowhere in sight. He called her and heard an answering cry, but she did not reappear.

He swore again. The rock must be hollow, and his bloody bird was in the middle of it. If he didn't catch her before she devoured her prey, he'd lose her as a hunting hawk. Bird be damned, but she was his best, and he was loath to lose her. If there was no other way in, he would have to climb.

Siward had not climbed rocks or trees since he was a boy, but he was not so old that he did not enjoy doing it again. Just as long as his grandmother or his future subjects didn't catch him behaving like a youth.

The rock had a surprising number of easy toeholds for him, so it wasn't long until Siward had reached the top. The view he saw from his vantage point, though, made his mouth fall open in surprise. What he had taken for a rock was in fact a sprawling building – he'd been climbing the walls. Astor, bright bird that she was, had perched on a wall that had partially fallen down, hiding her from his sight until now. He called her again, but the stubborn bird did not move.

Siward swore again. He would have to fetch her. At least it would be a simple matter of walking along the walls to her current spot, scooping her up and hooding her once more.

He could not keep his eyes on the bird and his footing, though, and by the time he looked up, the blasted bird had moved to a wall in the middle of the building. She teetered there for a moment, before diving into the room below.

Siward made his way to the spot where he'd last seen Astor, and stopped. Below him was a courtyard, free of the collapsed roof fragments most of the other rooms had sported. Yet it was not the courtyard that drew his eye, but the incredibly lifelike statue of a woman in the middle of it, surrounded by roses.

Made of alabaster or white marble, she looked as though she would open her eyes and rise at any moment. Some virgin goddess or the Queen of Heaven, Siward guessed, depending on how old the statue was. Yet it looked newly carved, not as though it had been lying in this ruin for centuries, as surely it had been. A wondrous work of art indeed.

If he had to take the throne, he would place this statue in the throne room, so that every time he was bored, he could stare at her and wonder what her story was, and remember how he'd found her on his last days of freedom.

Siward jumped down from the wall, bending his knees to cushion the impact of his landing. Good thing, too, for the ground beneath his feet was harder than he expected. Swiping his booted foot through the leaf litter, he pushed aside the thin layer to reveal a mosaic floor of remarkable craftsmanship, though it paled into insignificance when compared to the magnificent statue.

Now he was closer, she looked even more divine. Like his every desire made flesh – or stone, at least. Siward laughed at himself. A statue so real it stirred his loins. Perhaps becoming king would not be such a bad thing. He would be expected to take a queen, and ensure a clear succession. That would stop him from lusting after statues.

No, he decided, inspecting the goddess, for no real woman could look so perfect. He must have this statue in his throne room.

He reached out to touch the stone, to see what fastened her to the plinth below. Perhaps he could move her out of here and send someone to collect the statue, so that it would be in place when he returned.

If she had been fastened by her feet and fallen over at some point, he might be able to…

A briar shot out, twining around his wrist so fast he could not move it. "What in blazes – " he began, only now realising that the plants had sent tendrils around both of his legs and his other arm, too. A thicker branch snaked around his middle, yanking him away from the statue.

Siward shouted for help, but he was alone in the ruin, as he well knew.

No, not quite alone.

Astor, his traitorous bird, landed on the plinth beside the statue's shoulder and peered at the goddess' face, as though working out what her lips would taste like. That beak could chip stone, and ruin the statue. The bird had caused enough trouble today.

"No!" Siward commanded. "Leave the girl alone. She is not to be harmed."

Finally deciding to be obedient, the bird flew off, perching on the wall once more.

Siward breathed a sigh of relief. She was safe.

He thought he heard something rustling through the leaves, and turned his attention back to the statue. What he saw stole his breath and his voice.

For the statue's closed eyes now stood open, green as emeralds, as she stared back at him.

Twelve

Rosamond's mind drifted as she slumbered, dreaming of the endless cycle of the seasons as the plants around her grew, flourished or lay dormant, all the while whispering that they kept her safe. If such was her afterlife, she would not complain. Sometimes in her dreams she was a tree or bush herself, fighting the bite of an axe or blade as she defended her kingdom. Even if it was no longer hers in death.

Today, the dream was different. For a moment, she was a briar, defending herself from a fool who would bring plague to the kingdom, and the next, she had the limbs of a woman again, and eyes with which to see that he was no fool, but Sir Warin, brave knight that he was, trying to save her.

While she held him fast to the wall, out of reach, she directed her thoughts inward. If a single mote of the insidious plague lived inside her, she could not allow him to touch her and infect himself and others. But if the plague was gone and she yet lived…

Deep joy warmed her heart as she felt no trace of the disease within her.

Of course she would not. For she was dead, and this was merely a dream, like all the other times she had seen Sir Warin.

A dream where she could finally indulge her feelings for the knight whose life she'd saved.

With a thought, she released him from his bonds, healing the cuts the briars had inflicted, for she could reach through plants now without needing to touch him herself. She could do little with his shredded clothing, and she rather admired his well-muscled flesh she glimpsed through what remained of his tunic and hose.

What was it Queen Margareta had said? Let a man glimpse you naked, for he would do anything to see such beauty again. Rosamond had not realised the desire would run both ways – that she herself would want to see more of the man.

There was only one course of action, then.

"Come, my love," Rosamond said. "I have been waiting for you, for this moment. Take me as a bride on her wedding night, for soon we will be wed, and we have waited far too long already. The responsibility of the throne awaits, but for now, we should take pleasure in each other's arms. We must become one before others try to tear us apart."

He stumbled toward where she lay on her bed of roses, then took her hand and kissed it.

Rosamond tingled delightfully at his touch. Much better than their first awkward kiss by the campfire. But she burned for more. "Come to my bed, and love me," she said.

Warin climbed into the fountain beside her, then took her face in his hands and kissed her. This was no awkward peck like the first time. No, his lips moved with hers, parting so that they might share a breath before their tongues danced like the lovers they would soon be.

Warin paid no attention to the briars tearing the rags of his clothes from his body, until they both lay naked, and the desire burning between them was too much for either of them to resist. In her dreams, she had seen many things, including how a husband made love to his wife, and she wanted all this and more from her valiant knight.

"Love me," she commanded, parting her legs as she invited him inside.

Rosamond felt a sharp sting as he entered her, but it was no more than the prick of a thorn amid the overwhelming pleasure he gave her. Kisses and caresses were nothing...nothing, compared to this.

He made love to her as the sun set, and twilight settled over the land, so that when the first star sparkled in the sky and she cried out for joy once again, she could truly say she flew among the stars.

If only every awakening could be so joyful, but in her heart, Rosamond knew this could only be a dream.

Thirteen

Siward woke from a fevered dream. What kind of man dreamed he made love to a statue come to life? Or plants that moved like snakes, snaring and trapping him before the statue commanded them to stop?

He must have taken a stronger jug of wine than he'd thought. For only in his cups could he possibly place himself in such a silly fairy tale.

He stared up at the sky for a moment, reaching for the jug he knew should be beside him. All he touched were leaves, before pricking himself on a thorn. He had slept in a rosebush, then, instead of rolled in his cloak on the ground. He must do this again, for it felt far softer than the unforgiving ground. In fact, he could almost imagine the woman of his dreams beside him, pressing her breasts along his side as she reached for him once more.

"I see you are ready for me again, beloved," a distinctly female voice said, sounding amused as a warm, soft hand wrapped around his shaft. "Good. I wish you to love me again, just as you did last night."

Siward swallowed, then turned his head to meet her green eyes. The green eyes of a goddess, a divine statue come to life.

He bolted out of the bed, which he now saw was a fountain full of roses. He should have been covered in scratches from the thorns, but he was unscathed. A minor miracle, seeing as his clothes were little more than rags as he stood naked before a woman…nay, little more than a girl, who he had deflowered scant hours before.

Oh, he had done so at her command, which he could not refuse at the time, but now…honour demanded he make this right by her. That meant making her his wife.

He didn't even know her name.

"Are you real?" he asked.

The girl laughed. "I am no more or less real than you. Are you real?"

"Of course," he said firmly, trying not to be distracted by his body's response to her nakedness.

She was not so restrained. "Prove it. Come back to bed and love me again in daylight, or I shall fear last night was but a dream."

Siward shook his head. "I cannot. I should not have...I dishonoured you. I will make this right. I will take you as my wife, if you wish it."

"I do wish it, but I also wish for you to take me as you would your wife, here, now," the girl commanded imperiously.

No one in the kingdom commanded Lord Siward. Who was this slip of a girl who thought she could?

"Who are you?" Siward said.

The girl tossed her hair. "As if you do not know. I am Rosamond."

Named for the lost princess, like so many other girls in the kingdom, Siward thought. Every third woman under the age of fifty answered to the name Rose, for the princess had become legend.

He gave a wry smile. "Lying there like that, you look more like a goddess of love than a princess. You should be Freyja or Venus, not a mere princess."

Rosamond blushed redder than the roses around her. "You give pretty compliments. It is one of the many things I like about you. Of course, there is also your strength, your sense of honour and duty, your

74

prowess in battle, and now your prowess in bed. I shall list your virtues when we see my mother and father, so that they will consent to our marriage."

Siward almost smiled at her naiveté. No parent in the kingdom would refuse his offer of marriage for their daughter, especially once he claimed the throne for his own. Even if he hadn't deflowered their virgin daughter. He sighed. When he'd thought of taking a queen yesterday, he had not thought to make a decision already.

"Where are your clothes?" he asked.

She laughed softly. "You can probably answer that better than I can. I never took care of the horses."

Puzzled, he opened his mouth to ask for an explanation, but he closed it again when he realised his spare clothes were with his horse, too. Climbing out of here naked, with the walls full of briars, would not be without pain. He could save her a little of that, though, if he lifted her to the top of the wall. "Come here," he said. "I will help you get out of here, and then we can find you some clothes to wear."

Reluctantly, she sat up, wincing a little as though not accustomed to being upright. She shook her head slightly and slid her legs over the side of the fountain, so they dangled above the mosaic floor. Rosamond took a deep breath before she stood up. She remained on her feet for a moment, before her knees buckled and she would have crashed to the tiles if Siward had not leaped forward to catch her.

"I am sorry," she murmured, closing her eyes. "I must still be weak from lying so long abed. Forgive me."

Realisation dawned on Siward, and it was not a pleasant feeling. Her weakness was his fault, for last night had been her first time and he had not held back. No wonder the girl was weak. He'd been a brute. He lifted her in his arms, like the bride she would soon be, he swore. "If I lift you to the top of the wall, do you think you have the strength to stay there until I climb up to you?" he asked.

Rosamond rested her head against his chest. "Why are we climbing walls? The way out is that way." She pointed at a gap in the briars Siward had not seen before. Not that he'd been looking, he admitted, for his eyes had been too busy feasting on her beauty to notice anything else. She directed him through the ruin, following a path that was miraculously free of the briars that covered everything else. Almost as though someone had cleared it deliberately.

Surely delicate Rosamond had not done it. "Do you come here often?" he asked her.

She stared at him, as if he had made a joke. "No, this was my first visit."

"Do you live nearby?" he persisted. If she did, he

could ride by her parents' cottage to ask for her hand today. It would ease his conscience immeasurably.

"Of course not. I lived with my parents in the castle."

In a bigger kingdom, there might be more than one castle, but in a place this small, she could only mean the late king's castle. The one Siward's grandmother insisted should be his.

"Why have I not seen you there?" he asked.

"Perhaps because your duties keep you busy, and I prefer to spend as much time as possible in the gardens."

Siward could not recall ever seeing the castle gardens. She evidently knew him better than he knew her. If he had ever seen her before, he would have been just as transfixed as he'd been yesterday. More, perhaps, for a living woman was infinitely better than a cold stone statue.

"You must be right," he allowed.

Rosamond laughed. "I usually am."

She had the prideful manner of royalty already. Not a bad thing in a future queen. Perhaps destiny had led him to her yesterday, and played a hand in kindling their lust. Nothing else could explain his complete loss of control, Siward was certain of it. The only other explanation was…magic. And how could a girl so young be a witch? Siward wanted to laugh at the thought.

Destiny it must be, then. At least destiny favoured him.

"Where is my horse?" she demanded.

Siward had the distinct feeling that destiny was laughing at him, too.

Fourteen

Rosamond didn't want to admit it, but her illness had left her so weak she could scarcely walk. Delightful though it was to be carried in Sir Warin's arms, she had no desire to be known as the princess who swooned at the slightest excuse. As she'd slept, she'd mastered her gifts, so that she'd healed Warin's scratches even as he made love to her.

If only he'd taken the time to do it again this morning, once she realised this was no longer a dream. She lived, and she had successfully persuaded him to make her his wife. A wife who intended to take great delight in her marriage bed, for her husband knew how to please her.

Her return home should be proud and triumphant, as befitted a betrothed princess, but between her own frailty and the absence of her horse, she wasn't sure how she would achieve such a spectacle. Least of all in the hose and tunic Sir Warin tossed to her.

Of course she could hardly ride naked, but she'd had countless new gowns made for Queen Margareta's coronation. Surely Sir Warin could not have burned them all.

Yet…it seemed he had. Not only was all the cloth gone, but all her clothing, too. She toyed with the idea of sending him to the nearest town to procure something proper for a princess to wear, but that meant he would have to leave her alone here, for who knew how long?

No.

It was a set of his own ill-fitting garments or nothing. When they reached a town, then she would insist he find something to replace what he had burned.

He helped her dress, then lifted her onto the back of his palfrey. For a while, he walked beside the horse, with the reins wrapped around his hand, but when Rosamond came close to fainting in the summer heat, he mounted up behind her, and only his strong arms kept her from slipping out of the saddle.

"Rest, Rosamond. I shall keep you safe," he promised.

Sleepily, she nodded, and the rest of the journey passed in what she described as a blurry doze. Sometimes she opened her eyes to bright sunlight, and at others to starry darkness. The one constant was Sir Warin's reassuring presence, for even at night, he held her in his arms. Though his hands did not slide under her tunic even once, to her disappointment. She was too weak to properly enjoy the attention, she told herself. Once they were home in the castle, and she had recovered properly, then she would tell him to take her again and again until she was sated.

She drifted from dream to dream, waking only to dream again, until one morning she opened her eyes and saw the wooden beams of a ceiling instead of the sky above. Now she woke fully, aware of being alone in a bed, with no idea of how long she had been there.

"Hello?" she called, annoyed. "Monika? Sir Warin? Anyone?"

The door to the room opened and a maidservant entered, bowing her head. She was too young to be Monika. "They are not here, my lady," the girl said. "I have orders to serve you and see that you are well when the master returns. Is there anything I can bring you, my lady? Some wine, something to eat, or a physician? The master thought you might be ill."

"I am not ill," Rosamond snapped. As a healer, she was far more knowledgeable about such things than some stupid physician. "Bring me fruit, and meat, and yes, some wine. Then fetch me my clothes."

The girl dropped a deep curtsey. "Yes, my lady."

She returned some time later with a tray of food and drink. Rosamond did her best, but she could barely eat more than a few mouthfuls. The wine was much too strong, threatening to turn her stomach. She had eaten little on the journey, and she estimated that she had stayed in the ruined convent for perhaps a week, so perhaps her stomach had shrunk from eating so little. No matter. She would be back to normal in no time.

When she was certain she could not eat another bite, Rosamond said, "Where are my clothes? I must dress. I wish to sit in the garden."

"I will ask the housekeeper, my lady. She was still searching for your clothes when I brought your breakfast." The girl took the barely touched tray and hurried out.

When the girl returned, Rosamond had fallen into a doze, but she roused herself quickly. "Well?" Rosamond demanded.

"Draga says you had no things with you when you arrived, but she is looking through some of the chests of old clothes, to see if we have anything that will fit you, my lady."

Old clothes. Rosamond sniffed. When she was well once more, she would summon a dressmaker to make anew all the garments Sir Warin had burned. In the meantime...she would accept the housekeeper's charity, for it was surely the best the woman had. When she saw Sir Warin again, she would instruct him on how to treat a princess when she was a guest in his home, for she guessed she was in his house. She was certainly not in her parents' castle, for there was no stonework to be seen.

Two menservants entered the room, bearing an enormous chest between them. An older woman, who Rosamond assumed was Draga, the housekeeper, followed them.

Draga stood with her hands on her hips, eyeing Rosamond as though she was a piece of meat. "Skinny, with no hips to speak of. A poor choice in a wife, and I shall tell the master so."

Rosamond's temper flared. "Your master has better judgement than you. There is nothing wrong with my hips, as your master knows well." In fact, his hands had held her hips fast as he thrust deep into her, and she longed for him to do it again. "I hope you brought clothes befitting someone of my rank. I will not dress like a peasant, nor a man."

Draga's eyes flashed. "The clothes in that chest belonged to the Lady Schutz when she was a girl. Nothing else in the house will fit. If they are not good enough for you, then I suggest you return from whence you came and leave the master to find a proper wife, not one so full of airs and graces." Her eyes narrowed. "With no hips." She waved at the young maidservant. "Agnna, you take care of her highness. I have more important things to do." The housekeeper strode out of the room before Rosamond could form a reply to such breathtakingly bad manners.

At least the housekeeper had recognised her as a princess, Rosamond consoled herself, though the honorific had sounded more like an insult on Draga's lips. No matter. As the lady of the house, Rosamond could dismiss the woman and engage someone more appropriate, if she wished.

Agnna didn't seem to have noticed the housekeeper's rudeness. Perhaps the girl was used to it. She fell to her knees beside the chest and lifted the lid. "Lady Schutz always looks so lovely. I'm sure these gowns will be everything you could want, my lady," she breathed, drawing out the first one, a simple dress of black linen. Or was it dark grey? Rosamond could not be sure. The second gown the girl lifted out was a much more becoming shade of pink, though it, too, looked like it might have faded. "This is beautiful. I have never touched cloth so smooth."

That got Rosamond's attention. "Is it silk? Bring it here." She reached for the dress and was relieved to find that it was indeed silk. As were most of the dresses in the chest. Rosamond selected the gowns in shades of pink and green, before dismissing the rest as unsuitable. She breathed a sigh of relief. At least she would have something to wear until the castle dressmaker could create a new wardrobe befitting both a princess and Sir Warin's new bride.

For a bride she would be. He had asked, and she had accepted, and they had already consummated their union beneath the moonlight.

Her father would not refuse this match, she was certain of it. Especially not if she announced it to him herself before Sir Warin asked for her hand.

"Does my father know I am here?" Rosamond asked.

"I do not know, my lady. I can send word to him, if you wish. But surely he must know, for if you are to marry the master, he would have your father's blessing. He is very strict about matters of honour, is the master. There are tales of maids in other households being…dishonoured, but you will never hear of such a thing here." Agnna sounded quite proud of this.

"Is that because the dragon of a housekeeper does

not allow the servants to spread such vicious rumours?" Rosamond asked.

Agnna clapped a hand to her mouth to smother a giggle. "No, my lady, and her name is Draga, not dragon, though when she is angry, sometimes I think she might breathe fire, she is so fearsome. They are more than rumours. Why, Lord Vamos has sent away four kitchen maids this year alone. All pregnant, and all unwed. Some say it is the lord himself who does the deed, but others whisper that it is his son, Fodor."

"A lord and his son who seduce the women of their household, pledging their love with no intention of marrying the girls? Who would do such a thing? Surely, honour cannot be so dead!" Rosamond exclaimed.

"My lady, there is little of love when a man desires a woman. It is different with the master, for what woman would not want him? High and honourable as he is, I do not believe he would seduce a woman without marriage on his mind. But any other nobleman...if he wishes to bed one of his servants, the girl has no choice but to obey. I heard that Moxa, Lady Vamos' maid, tried to refuse, but they beat her so badly that in the end she begged Fodor to take her so the beatings would stop. She still lost her position, and none will employ a fallen woman."

"Fallen? Or forced?" Rosamond asked sharply.

Agnna shrugged. "There is little difference in the

law of the land. It protects noblemen, not us."

"When I am queen, I will change that," Rosamond vowed. "No woman should be forced to lie with a man against her will. It is barbaric."

"I wish you every blessing in your endeavour, my lady," Agnna said. "But…better not to speak of such things to the master for a while yet. He has so many other, more important cares on his shoulders nowadays, what with being Lord Protector and all. Best to pay attention to making him happy and saving your strength for the wedding." She looked up at Rosamond. "Will you need my help dressing, my lady?"

"No," Rosamond replied. "I think I still need to rest a little longer. Perhaps tomorrow. You may go."

The girl left the room, but Rosamond was so deep in thought she barely noticed. Before, Rosamond had believed that being queen was an irritating obligation, and marrying well would allow her to leave ruling up to her husband. No more. Not if women were being raped by the very noblemen the kingdom depended on to protect the people.

Lord Vamos, his son and any other man who thought women were chattels to be used and thrown away were in for a rude shock when she ascended the throne. For the first time in her life, she looked forward to her coronation.

Rosamond waited for Warin to visit her, but there was no sign of him, and when she asked Agnna about her master's whereabouts, the girl simply said she did not know.

Patience had never been Rosamond's strong point, so after two days abed, she decided to try walking again. Slowly at first, holding onto the bed for a few steps before she needed to sit down again, then a little longer each time until she could walk about the room without needing a rest. She needed to speak to her father before Warin did, for even if he had been named Lord Protector – a prestigious promotion for a captain of the guard – her parents had wanted her to marry some foreign prince.

She simply had to convince them that Warin was the better choice. But first, she had to regain her strength, and the fastest way to do that involved spending time in Warin's garden, if she could find it. If not, she could always cuddle up to the nearest tree. A mighty oak did not have the ebullience of something faster growing like a rose or berry bush, but she did not need to borrow much energy for what was more a tonic than proper healing.

Cautiously, Rosamond made her way downstairs. The bedchambers were on the highest floor of the house, above the great hall, with the kitchens and servants' quarters in the partially subterranean lowest level, she discovered as she descended.

A mob of wide eyes greeted her as she reached what must have been the servants' dining hall.

"What are you doing here, my lady?" Agnna asked, no less surprised than the rest.

A princess did not apologise to those lower than her, Rosamond remembered, as if her mother was even now hissing the words into her ear. Rosamond lifted her chin. "Looking for a garden to sit in."

"The master does not have a garden to speak of,

my lady, unless you count the kitchen garden, with the herbs and vegetables…"

"Or the orchard," a young boy piped up. "I'm supposed to pick the ripe ones from the berry patch this afternoon, but there's still plenty for you, my lady."

Berry bushes, the next closest thing to roses. "That sounds wonderful. Will you show me?"

The boy nodded happily before bounding up the steps too fast for Rosamond to follow.

"I will take you, my lady," Agnna said, proceeding at a much slower pace up the stairs. "If you will follow me? Someone will bring you refreshment, for you will need it outside in the summer heat."

The servants' quarters of Warin's house were far more confining than those in the castle, but then his house was so much smaller. Not as tiny as one of the peasant cottages she'd passed on the road, but still…much smaller than she was accustomed to. The walled garden Agnna led her to did not disappoint, though, for the orchard surpassed the small copse of trees in the castle garden by a considerable quantity.

Not to mention Rosamond spotted…

"Cloudberries!" she exclaimed. "I did not know there were any in the kingdom."

"I believe these are the only ones," Agnna said. "The master's grandfather brought the seeds back from foreign lands in his youth and planted them here. While the other, more common berries may be eaten by all, those yellow ones are reserved for the lord's table alone."

"I look forward to tasting them again," Rosamond said. She dropped to her knees and reached for the nearest plant, whose flowers were just beginning to open. The leaves curled up to touch her fingers, like a cat begging to be stroked. "I predict a bountiful crop of cloudberries this year." As she caressed the leaves, she felt the plants' delighted acquiescence to her desire for more berries.

"They are called princess berries here, my lady, on account of the lost princess. The master's grandfather travelled with her until she was lost. The berry seeds were a gift to her from some foreign queen, but when m'lord's grandfather brought her things to the king and told him of her loss, the king refused to allow the queen's gifts in the castle, swearing they were cursed, like the other gifts the evil queen gave the princess before she died. So he planted them here instead, in her memory."

This was a story Rosamond had not heard before. Perhaps her nursemaids had not thought it fit for a young princess's ears, to hear the grisly fate of one of her ancestors. Curses could be as cruel as their casters. Yet Agnna knew the story. "How did she die?"

Rosamond asked.

Agnna shrugged. "No one knows. The curse took her, m'lord's grandfather used to say. She lay like a marble statue in the garden, and the plants would attack those who tried to reach her. He called and called, but she did not wake, and that's how he knew she was dead."

A princess gifted with plant magic, just like her, Rosamond thought, pleased. Not that it had served her particularly well, but even Rosamond's own modest powers were no match for a powerful enchantress, as the evil queen must have been. Margareta had been a much more pleasant monarch.

"Tell me more about the plants in this garden," Rosamond ordered. She only half-listened to the girl's rambling as she trailed her fingers through everything green she could touch, for the plants themselves whispered a far more complex history than any human could.

Sixteen

Siward rode through the outlying villages in a sort of fog, though the air was clear. No, the fog was in his head. Green-eyed and smiling, the mysterious Rosamond haunted him by day and lay beside him in his dreams. Well, not always beside him. Sometimes beneath him and one particularly tantalising time she sat astride him, but…

Siward shook his head. He was supposed to be listening to petitions from the villagers, making judgements and settling disputes. Not thinking about bedding the beautiful woman who had agreed to be his wife. He had another week or two of this before he could head home to see her again.

It had sat ill with him to leave her alone in his house, with no one but his servants for company, but she had been too weak to even open her eyes when he'd laid her in his bed and kissed her farewell. A chaste kiss, for all he wanted more, because an honourable man did not steal so much as a kiss from a sleeping woman.

He did not doubt that his household would care for her as best they could, but they had not ridden miles with her lolling lifelessly in their arms, as he had. Yet she'd seemed so strong and vital that first night in his arms, crying out for more until he granted her desire.

He refused to regret it. Their one night of passion would allow him to take that beautiful creature as his willing wife. More than he deserved, perhaps, which was why he worried now. Destiny had given her to him, but if cruel fate saw fit to steal her away from him so soon...

Siward prayed that she would regain her strength in his house, instead of wasting away to nothing. Perhaps the place he had found her was magical, granting her strength that waned the further she travelled away from it.

No, that could not be true. She had nearly fallen when she'd first tried to stand up. He could scarcely wait to go home, when he hoped she would fall into his arms again. Not from weakness, but from sheer joy at seeing him again. Siward had to laugh at himself for that foolish thought. How could he bring a girl joy when he'd barely known her for a night? A night where they'd had little time or breath for conversation.

Yet he knew if she asked him to, he would claim the crown for her. There was no doubt in his mind that she would make the perfect queen. Gracious and beautiful, fearless yet soulful...no wonder she was always in his thoughts.

Every glimpse of green reminded him of her eyes. Every time a leaf brushed against him, he thought of the night they'd shared in their bed of roses.

Finally, he made his last judgement at Akos, a tiny village at the foot of the mountains that marked the kingdom's easternmost boundary. Though they offered him hospitality for the night, Siward refused, wishing to sleep in the forest instead. Not that he told the village headman that, of course. He told the man he was needed in the capital, to solve the matter of the succession. An excuse that had the virtue of being true.

He waved to the townspeople as he rode off, his saddlebags filled with provisions he did not need but could not refuse. Siward intended to spend the night in a small dell he had found on his way to Akos, where the soft grass had cushioned him as he spent the night enchanted by vivid dreams of Rosamond.

Soon, he promised himself, he would be home. They would be wed and he could do all the things he'd dreamed about with his very real wife instead of his illusory goddess.

Seventeen

Slowly but surely, Rosamond regained her strength. The garden bloomed as happily as she did. More than once, she had overheard the servants talking about it, but she refused to be deterred by idle talk. When she saw her father again, she wanted to appear as hale and healthful as the day she departed for King Erik and Queen Margareta's court.

After four weeks of spending every day in the garden, Rosamond decided it was time. On the morrow, she would don her finest gown – or at least the least faded gown in the chest of old clothes Draga had foisted on her – and proceed up to the palace, where she would seek an audience with the king and queen, and explain her plan for the future.

The best of intentions rarely survive until morning, especially when illness sets in. Rosamond's improving appetite disappeared overnight, and what she did manage to swallow she only threw right back up again. She felt dizzy and weak, as she had when she had first arrived.

Rosamond had no more time for weakness, she decided, as she dragged herself outside to the garden. Reaching deep into a bramble bush, she let the thorns pierce her skin as she commanded the plant to help her heal herself.

Her heart beat loud in her ears, as it always did when she attempted magic on herself, deafening her to all other sound. Or it should have, but for an eager thrumming she had never heard before. What was it? she asked the plants as she searched for the source. The answers she received sounded like saplings and seeds, which made no sense. No plant she knew sounded like a rapidly beating heart.

And then she knew. Reaching deep inside herself, Rosamond found the sound's source. A heart so tiny she could scarcely see it, but a human heart nonetheless. Within her, she carried Warin's child – and, after her, the next heir to the throne.

Eighteen

Contrary to his usual custom, Siward left his horse to his groom's care instead of caring for the animal himself. It had been eight weeks…nay, fifty-eight days since he had last seen Rosamond, and he longed for her the same way the first spring flowers sought the sun. He needed her.

Draga greeted him in the great hall, asking inane questions about what he wanted prepared for dinner. Siward waved away her concerns, for he had only one thought in his head.

"How is she? Where is she?" he asked eagerly.

Draga's brow creased. "The sick girl you brought?"

Siward prayed with all his might that she was not still ill. "Rosamond."

"She's in the garden. She's always in the garden," Draga said.

Exactly where she should be, Siward thought as he bolted for the door. It was the height of summer, and everything bloomed so brightly he didn't see her at first. The green gown and white shift she wore underneath blended so well with the leaves and blossoms behind her that he might have missed her entirely had she not moved.

Her face lit up with joy, just as he'd imagined it would. He raced across the garden and swept her into his arms, heedless of who saw as he kissed her with more passion than he'd ever shown anyone else in his life.

Siward wanted more. He wanted to throw her to the ground, tear off her gown and make love to her like he had every night in his dreams, but he knew he could not do such a thing. Not to her. Her body yielded to him so readily even now that he did not dare abuse her trust. Not again. He would not take her to bed until they were properly married, he swore.

"You are home sooner than I thought. Your servants said it would be another two weeks at least," she said, her smile lighting up the morning brighter than the sun.

"I could not stay away from you," he confessed. "I want us to be wed as soon as possible. Tomorrow, if we can."

She drew away from him, bowing her head. "First, I must speak to my father."

Of course! In his eagerness, how could he have forgotten? "I will speak to him. I will ask for your hand and all will be well." No father in the kingdom would refuse him, Siward knew. "What is his name? I shall summon him, and we shall have his answer before nightfall."

This did not please Rosamond, who shook her head violently. "You cannot summon him. Not my father. I must speak to him, and only then can you ask him for anything."

Perhaps her father was a nobleman who thought to claim the kingship for himself. A man with such pride would not agree to Siward's suit until his future son-in-law sat firmly on the throne. So be it. There was nothing he would not do for her, and ruling a kingdom was a small price to pay for happiness with her.

"It shall be as you say," he conceded. "On the morrow, I will go to the castle to attend to some important business, while you speak to your father. Once my business and your conversation are concluded, then I will speak to him. We will be happily wed before this summer is over, I promise."

"I believe you."

She did not leave his side for the rest of the day. Even at supper, they shared a bench, while Draga muttered under her breath. Siward wanted to laugh – surely his housekeeper had been in love before. If she had, she would understand the bond between him and his betrothed.

It felt almost painful to part with her to go to separate sleeping chambers, but he forced himself to do no more than kiss her good night before vanishing into one of the seldom-used guest chambers. After all, he consoled himself, she would invade his dreams the moment his eyes closed.

He did not have to wait long. Sleep stole over him like a magic spell, where the witch was his wife-to-be and he would not have it any other way.

Nineteen

Rosamond refused to sleep alone once Warin had returned. She belonged in his bed, and she'd seen her own desire mirrored in his eyes from the moment he arrived. So she waited until she thought he was asleep, and crept into his bedchamber. Shucking off her shift, she slid under the blankets beside him.

She took his hands in hers and placed them on her body, stroking his fingers along her skin until he took control and caressed her on his own. His soft kisses turned hungry as his hands pushed her legs apart, just like she wanted him to, before he thrust deep inside her.

Rosamond gasped in surprise and pleasure. Tonight, he needed no urging as he drove her to heights of pleasure she had never known before, not just once but over and over until her frenzied cries mingled with his.

When they were both sated, she wanted nothing more than to fall asleep in his arms, but Rosamond knew she must return to her own chamber, at least until they were wed. She needed to be well-rested for her interview with her father on the morrow.

Twenty

"So we are all in agreement, then? Until we find a way to break down the Wall, or another claimant with a more direct line of descent from the royal family makes himself known, Lord Siward shall be king."

Siward blinked, not sure he had heard Lord Vamos correctly. For as long as he could remember, and as recently as the last time the King's Council convened, Lord Vamos had been his most vocal opponent. His claim to the throne had been tenuous at best – a bastard he claimed was a by-blow of the king's, three or four generations into the past. Lord Vamos didn't even have proof of his claim, for the bastard girl had never been acknowledged by her royal father, and the child she'd borne her husband might have been a bastard, too, if the current lord's senescent great-grandfather had not decided to marry her scant weeks before taking to his deathbed. Which begged the question of whether the current lord's grandfather had been conceived in his father's deathbed...

Yet here the man was, turning himself inside out to support Siward's claim to the throne. It almost made Siward want to refuse, for Lord Vamos would as soon hand him a cup of poison as a cup of wine.

Nods and murmurs of assent issued from the men clustered around the table.

Lord Vamos slapped his hand on the table. "It is decided, then. Siward shall be king, provided he can produce an heir within a year of his coronation."

Ah, there was the rub. Siward was the only man among them who did not have a son, or a wife by which he could beget more. Fortune favoured him, for that would soon change.

Siward rose. "With a heavy heart, I accept the honour of being your king, gentlemen. Let us set as early a date as possible for my coronation. The kingdom has been without a king for long enough."

Lord Vamos flashed a smile that reminded Siward of a snake. "It has been without a queen for even longer. Unless you have a wife tucked away somewhere secret, I suggest – "

Siward held up his hands for silence. "I have already chosen my queen, my lords. As your king, I will do everything in my power to ensure the security and the succession in our kingdom. If the Wall ever comes down, though this summer it seemed stronger than ever, our neighbours will find us secure in our monarchy, with no need to look outside our borders for some distant relative of the late king. He named me Regent on his deathbed, as you all know, but I never thought then that I would be safeguarding the throne for myself. I thank you for your faith in me, my lords." He inclined his head, far from the usual bow he would have given these men before today, but a king bowed to no one. He might not be king yet, but in their minds, he must appear to be. With an imperious wave, he dismissed them.

Twenty-One

Rosamond's morning sickness returned with a vengeance on the morrow, as if to punish her for spending the night in her husband-to-be's bed. She endured it, as she knew she must, until finally she managed to choke down some small cider that did not immediately come back up.

With Agnna's assistance, she dressed in a pink gown that reminded her of the one she'd worn to the tournament on the day Warin had won the melee. A fitting gown to wear to the palace, where she would do battle with her father for the right to marry Warin.

As it was almost noon, Rosamond decided to attempt to eat the noonday meal before she left. She would feel far better with a full stomach than an empty one, she knew.

Feeling every inch the princess, Rosamond announced that she would take her meal in the garden instead of the great hall. Draga muttered under her breath, then headed down to the kitchen to obey her order.

Rosamond breathed deeply as she stepped outside into the sunshine, where Warin's happy garden awaited her company. She brushed her fingers through their leaves as she passed, drawing strength from their affection. She would need all the strength she possessed to win this encounter, and win she must.

Twenty-Two

Siward stopped at the door to his grandmother's cottage to take a deep breath. She was but a frail old woman, and no threat to anyone, he told himself, but he knew it was a lie. She could flay a man alive with her sharp tongue alone, and every maiden in the kingdom was terrified of her. Some called her a witch, but never to her face, lest Lady Schutz put an evil spell on them.

He knew there was no truth to her being a witch. His grandmother silenced him at the mere mention of magic, for in cursing the princess, the evil queen had cursed her, too. Cursed her to a life where she no longer had a position, for she had no mistress, and no other lady in the kingdom would dare to employ the lady-in-waiting who had served the princess, for how could any woman ever measure up to her? The princess was a veritable paragon of virtue, so the stories said, she had surely become a saint. The queen took pity on her for a time, and Grandmother became the queen's companion, but losing her daughter had broken the queen's heart, and she did not long survive the girl. So his grandmother, without a position once more, had married his grandfather and bore him some children including Siward's own father, which had led to the birth of Siward himself.

Which still didn't help him find the courage to raise his fist and knock on the formidable old lady's door. Luckily for him, the door flew open and Cecilia, a maid from his own household, stepped out. She gave a little start of surprise before she curtsied to him. "Have you come to visit Lady Schutz, master? I shall tell her you are here."

Siward nodded and followed the girl inside. He needed no introduction, after all. He would stay long enough to tell his grandmother that the Council had accepted his claim to the crown, and that he had chosen his queen. Grandmother would be too busy planning his coronation to spare a thought for

Rosamond.

Yes, that was the plan.

She greeted him with, "So, have you come to tell me the date of your coronation?"

Of course she already knew. Word travelled fast in a town this size, especially to a woman like her who had spent half her life in the castle.

"On St John's Eve," Siward replied. "Soon, for the kingdom is in need of a leader, and I will not let it wait any longer."

"You must take a bride, too," Lady Schutz said, nodding. "The sooner, the better. For the naysayers will not rest until you put a babe in her belly. And I know just the one."

"So do I," Siward began, but she didn't let him finish.

"Lord Vamos' daughter, Jolanka. She is young, obedient and definitely fertile." Grandmother beamed. "She will make a good wife for you."

Lord Vamos' daughter? Now Siward knew why the man had agreed to giving him the crown. He had made some sort of deal with his grandmother so that his daughter could be queen. Yet no matter how much he racked his brain, Siward could not recall seeing a young woman any time he had visited the man's house. And the way Grandmother stressed her fertility…

"Is the Lady Jolanka newly widowed?" he guessed.

Grandmother snorted. "The girl is barely fourteen summers old. Old enough to be a bride. Your bride."

But for her to be fertile… "She was his price, wasn't she? You told him I would take Lord Vamos' dishonoured daughter, perhaps even her bastard child, if he would give me the crown."

"Everything comes at a price," Grandmother said sharply. "The girl is a small price to pay. Lord Vamos sang her virtues, swearing that he did not know how the girl had begotten a bastard, for she never left her brother's side, and Fodor would defend her with his life."

Likely Fodor had drunk too much wine and defiled the girl himself, Siward fumed. He knew the man too well, and while Lord Vamos would not have made a terrible king, there was no way he would allow the crown to pass to a rabid dog like Fodor.

"Her brother will, of course, come with her to the castle, to be the captain of the queen's guard," Grandmother continued.

Even if Siward had considered the possibility of marrying the poor girl, there was no way he would tolerate her brother. Not to mention…he would have no way of knowing whether the girl's children were his or the result of incest and rape.

No, Rosamond would make a far better queen, and he could save Jolanka from her family some other way.

As king, he could arrange a suitable marriage for her to someone else on the other side of the kingdom from Lord Vamos and his odious son.

"Thank you for your advice, Grandmother. I will consider it when I choose my bride, but I suspect I will prefer someone with a little more experience than a sheltered fourteen-year-old for my queen. I will not keep you or the kingdom in suspense, for I plan to wed the same day as my coronation, on St John's Eve. An auspicious time for fertility, or so I have heard." Siward farewelled his grandmother, telling her he had matters of state to attend to in the castle for the rest of the day, before beating a hasty retreat.

Twenty-Three

Today, Rosamond's morning sickness turned into morning, noon and night sickness. There was no way she could go to the palace in this condition, let along argue Warin's suit. She lay among the cloudberries, with scarcely the strength to sit up. Slowly but surely, her dizziness receded so that she could stare at the nearest cloudberry bush and wonder if it had quite that many blossoms on it when she'd first lain beside it.

When she reached out a finger to stroke the petals, she received a smug burst of satisfaction from the plant. The new blossoms were its celebration of her returning health. Rosamond couldn't help it. She laughed aloud.

"So you are the crazy hedge witch my grandson brought home," a cold female voice said. "They say he plans to marry you, nobody that you are. He could choose any eligible maiden in the kingdom, you know. In fact, he's already all but betrothed to a lady far more highborn than you, a circumstance which he has apparently forgotten. But you shall remind him, when you break the spell you have cast on him."

Rosamond wanted to laugh some more, for the woman's words were surely a joke, yet she sounded deadly serious. Cautiously, she sat up, praying that her morning sickness was done torturing her for today. "I don't know what you're talking about," Rosamond said.

"Don't be ridiculous. Servants talk. Everyone in this household has seen and heard you talking to these plants. You have done something to them, just as you have magicked my grandson," the old lady snapped. "I demand you take it off."

"Take what off?" Rosamond asked tiredly. "My gown?"

"The spell you cast on my grandson, of course!" The woman glared. "But now I think about it, yes, you should also remove that gown. It is far too valuable for the likes of you. Why, that was worn by a princess to a queen's coronation. Look at it now – covered in dirt by some peasant woman who does not know good silk when she sees it!"

"Tournament, not coronation," Rosamond said absently. "This is not formal enough to be worn to a full coronation in court. This is the style of afternoon gown a highborn lady wears to a tournament. Like the one where Sir Warin won the melee." She rose to her feet, not willing to face this woman at a height disadvantage. No one stood higher than a princess except the queen. Sometimes not even then.

"I…how do you know that?" The woman peered at her.

Rosamond flashed a brilliant, courtly smile that had all the sincerity of cesspool slime. "I know many things. And whatever spells I may have cast, I will not undo. Not for you." The only spells she could cast were healing ones, anyway. What grudge did this woman bear against Warin that she wanted him not to be healed?

"You are a lowborn, ignorant hedge witch who has placed my grandson under a spell so that he believes himself in love with you. You shall remove it, or I shall summon the guards, and you shall be charged with treason!" the strange woman shrieked.

Rosamond drew herself up. "You are a rude, stupid old woman who knows nothing, least of all how to behave when speaking to someone of my rank. Remove yourself from my sight before I summon the servants to do it for you." She was proud of the fact that her voice remained cold and calm to the end, without a hint of her anger peeping through.

The rude, stupid old woman drew her hand back and slapped Rosamond across the face so hard she sent the princess tumbling to the ground.

Twenty-Four

Siward arrived home just in time to witness Rosamond's meeting with Lady Schutz. His instincts drove him to dive between the two women, defending Rosamond, but he held himself back. If she was to be his queen, she would need to know how to respond to courtiers. Plus, he had to admit, he wanted to hear her defence for himself. He knew there had been magic in the air in the ruins, but he would bet his life that it was not of her making.

Interesting. She did not deny the charge of being a witch, or of casting spells. Neither did she confirm

Grandmother's suspicions. Her regal response to the old lady's insults made him want to applaud. Oh, Rosamond was born to be queen.

But when Grandmother raised her hand to the girl, Siward did not move fast enough to prevent the blow. When she fell to the ground, his heart felt like it had dropped right out of his chest.

"Rosamond, are you all right?" he asked.

Lady Schutz batted at his shoulder. "Get away from the witch. She will curse you, boy. Worse than she already has. Throw her out of your house and into a dungeon."

Siward had no time for the old woman's hysterics.

"This woman will be my wife, and your future queen. In fact, she's already carrying my child, the next heir to this kingdom," Siward boasted, hoping his grandmother would not spot that this last was a lie. "If you ever attempt to strike her again, I will send you to a dungeon."

Lady Schutz gasped in horror. "Your own flesh and blood! After all I have done for you. You would not dare, boy!"

"Try me, Grandmother. I will marry Rosamond on St John's Eve and there is nothing you can do to stop me. Now get out."

Grandmother drew herself up. "Rosamond, is it? You don't deserve that name just as you do not deserve my grandson. Mark my words, slut: you will never be queen." She turned on her heel, nose in the air, and stormed out of Siward's house.

Siward stared after her for a moment, before he realised Rosamond still lay on the ground where she'd fallen. He hurried to help her up, checking her for injuries, but she assured him she was fine.

She did not look fine, though. She had dirt all over her gown and a frown that made his heart ache.

"Tell me what is wrong!" he implored.

"St John's Eve is so far away," she said slowly. "Almost a year. I would prefer to be wed well before then."

Now it was Siward's turn to frown in puzzlement. "No, St John's Eve is only a few weeks away."

Rosamond shook her head. "I distinctly remember Queen Margareta's coronation was on St John's Eve. The townspeople had bonfires burning in the town square and when I took fright at what I thought was a man ablaze on one, you told me he was made of wicker and not to worry. I refused to continue until I was certain that you were right. You were, but…I had horrible nightmares that night, of how it would feel to burn."

None of what she said made any sense, but Siward chose not to tell her so. She must have hit her head when she fell, scrambling her wits. "I shall take you to bed," he said, lifting her in his arms.

Those green eyes shone as she gazed up at him. "This is why I don't understand your desire to delay our nuptials. Don't you want me in your bed as much as I need you in mine?"

His loins stirred at her words, willing him to say yes, but Siward had long ago learned to control such urges. "To rest," he said softly. "I shall take you to bed so that you may rest."

She struggled in his grasp until he was forced to set her on her feet. "I don't want to rest. I've been doing nothing all day. Now, I need to change my gown so I can speak to my father, to prepare him before you ask for my hand."

Ah, yes. Something else he had to do before St John's Eve. "I shall go with you," Siward said.

She stared at him for a long moment, her lips parted as though she wished to argue. Then she lowered her eyes and nodded. "If you wish."

Twenty-Five

Rosamond rummaged through the chest of clothes in her chamber. Before, she had given the gowns little more than a cursory glance as she dressed each morning. But now, she laid them out on the bed one by one and truly examined them. What she found frightened her.

Mixed in with gowns she did not recognise were ones she most definitely did. The soiled gown she had worn today wasn't just like the one she'd worn to the tournament – it seemed to be the same gown, only faded from vibrant strawberry to a dusky rose. The gown she'd worn to Queen Margareta's coronation was more peach than pink now, for it had yellowed somehow. Faded, yellowed and, in one case, frayed where the lacings had come apart, as if with age. She did not understand how it was possible. How had Warin brought her things to his home while he was still in the convent with her? Where was Monika, then, and why did he not send for her? And why did he seem to think that it was still June when it was surely July?

Rosamond sank to her knees on the floor beside the empty chest. Only...it wasn't empty yet. A box she hadn't seen before, possibly because it was the same colour as the base of the chest, remained. She lifted it out, and opened it.

Inside lay Queen Margareta's rose crown, as fresh as the day it was picked, though the flowers should be long dead and dried after so many weeks of travel. First the faded gowns and now this. Rosamond didn't know what to think.

She felt bile rise up in her throat that had nothing to do with morning sickness. Not this time.

Rosamond did not know how long she sat there, her mind whirling with impossible explanations. No matter which one she tried to settle on, none of them made sense.

She wasn't sure how long Warin stood watching her

before he spoke. "What is that? Did you make it in the garden today?" He nodded toward the crown.

Something else that didn't make sense. "No," she said slowly. "Queen Margareta wore this to her coronation, and afterward, she gave it to me. This travelled with us until we stopped at the convent, where I did not see it again until I found it here, in a box of my clothes."

Warin closed the chest and perched on top of it. "I never heard of a queen by that name. Was she the one before Queen Maria?"

"No. She was crowned only a few weeks ago. You were there. You fought in the melee and won, before you knelt before her to claim victory. Even though you had a broken arm, you still won." She stared up at him. "That's when I knew you were the only man I could trust to protect me, no matter what happened. And I healed you." Rosamond moistened her lips. "Don't you remember?"

"You must have hit your head when you fell," he said. "Let me help you to bed, and on the morrow…"

"Don't you remember?" she repeated, more urgently this time.

"Rosamond, you're not well."

She jumped to her feet. "Answer me, Warin. Why don't you remember the queen?"

He stared back at her, impassive. "I don't

remember a queen because I've never seen one. Queen Maria died soon after her daughter, nigh on fifty years ago now, and King Almos never really had the heart to replace her. And, what with the Wall and all, he couldn't really go looking for a new wife, now, could he?"

Never seen a queen? Not possible. Unless...

Realisation dawned, turning into horror.

"You're not Sir Warin," Rosamond choked out. "You have all my things, and you look like him, but you're not him. Who are you?"

Twenty-Six

Siward's heart sank. He'd known all along this was too good to be true. A beautiful woman waiting for him, inviting him into her bed, where he was unable to resist her charms. She'd been waiting for someone else.

He rose. "I am Siward, Lord Protector of the Realm and Regent appointed by the king until a suitable heir is found. By my count, for only a few weeks more." Siward bowed low before her.

Her lips moved, but no sound came out. "Regent? But…what is wrong with the king?"

Did she truly not know? "He died," Siward said

gently. "Just this spring. He was an old man, and he rarely left his bed. He passed peacefully in his sleep, but not before he named me Regent."

"How long ago did the queen die?" she whispered.

"Almost fifty years ago now. Before my father was born, and after the Wall closed us in," Siward said.

"What of Sir Warin?" Her voice was so quiet now it was barely audible.

"If by Sir Warin, you mean my grandfather, who was the captain of the guard who lost the princess, he died when I was a boy, but not before he told me every story he knew." Siward swallowed. "He had one regret in his life, and he spoke of it more and more as he got older. He wished he'd found a way to save her."

Rosamond didn't seem to be listening any more. Her eyes had a faraway look. "How long did I sleep?"

Siward scratched his head. "I don't rightly know. You were asleep when I found you, just before you woke."

"Did Sir Warin tell you how long ago he lost his princess?" Her voice shook as her eyes filled with tears.

Siward considered his words before he spoke. "She was never his princess. Too high for him, and he knew it. He was just a captain of the guard. He would have given his life for her, if he could. She was his charge, and he failed her."

Tears spilled down her cheeks. "How long?"

He relented. "Fifty years."

She started to sob.

Siward had no idea why she was crying – what was so sad about some princess who'd been dead for fifty years? – but he could at least try to comfort her. He opened his arms to her and held her close while sobs shook her body for what seemed an eternity.

Finally, the storm seemed to subside and she mumbled something into his tunic.

Cautiously, he asked her to repeat it.

"Release me," she ordered.

He complied.

She straightened, wiped the tears from her face and managed to look every inch the queen he wanted her to be. "How dare you," she said, her voice shaking with fury now. "You pretended to be another man to make me feel affection for you, stole my maidenhead, and only now you tell me the truth? Your grandfather was a good man and an honourable one, but he would turn over in his grave if he knew what you have become."

"I stole nothing you did not give me freely," Siward shot back. "You opened your arms and your legs and all but begged me to climb into your bed. You never asked my name, and I never pretended to be anyone but myself. What kind of woman waits naked in the woods, anyway? Not an honourable one, that's for certain."

If anything, this only enflamed her further. "When I took to my bed, I was clothed as modestly as I am now. You know nothing about honour, or what I have endured." Green eyes blazed.

Siward spread his hands wide in invitation. "Tell me, then. Make me understand."

She gave a slight nod. "Very well. The day I went to sleep, I was dying of a plague picked up shortly after King Erik and Queen Margareta's coronation. Two of my travelling companions were struck down with it, too. I managed to heal them both, but not myself, so I barricaded myself in that courtyard and lay down to die. If what you tell me is true, fifty years I lay there, dreaming without waking, as my body slowly rid itself of the deadly disease and everyone I knew and loved died. Until the day you woke me."

No. She couldn't be. If the princess were still alive, she'd be more than sixty years old. Nothing like the stunning beauty before him, who didn't look a day older than twenty. It wasn't possible.

Steadily, she continued, "Then I was Crown Princess Rosamond, daughter of King Almos and Queen Maria. Now...I am your queen."

Twenty-Seven

The strange man who looked like Warin – Siward, was that what he'd said his name was? – didn't look particularly impressed by her announcement. Weren't men supposed to bow to their queen?

"Well? Aren't you going to say something?" Rosamond said finally, exasperated.

"You did hit your head," Siward said drily.

She blew out an angry breath. "You mean you don't believe me? You think instead that I am mad, or making this up? You said it yourself – why would a maiden wait in the woods without her clothes? Well, I gave you my answer. I slept for fifty years, safe until you broke into my bower."

"Even if you are the lost princess, no one will believe you. Even I am not sure if I believe you. You should be the same age as my grandmother, not standing before me, looking younger than I am." Siward shook his head. "If I were to place you on the throne today, the King's Council would declare that I am mad, and give the throne to someone else."

"They would try to steal my throne from me?" The very thought made her shake, though with fear or fury, she was not sure.

Siward laughed. "No, for none of them would believe it's yours in the first place. They would steal it from me."

She bristled. "So you steal not only my maidenhead, but my throne as well?"

"Enough with this this stealing nonsense!" he snapped. "No matter who you thought I was, you ordered me to make love to you, and I did. Several times. The king has been dead for weeks now, with no clear heir anywhere in the kingdom. I have searched, but still found no one who could take his place." When Rosamond opened her mouth to protest, he held up his hand to stop her. "Let me finish. Until a few minutes ago, I believed no one in the kingdom had a claim to the throne. That is why the King's

Council decided this morning to crown me as king on St John's Eve."

"But you believe me now?" she ventured, feeling hope blossom in her chest.

Siward's expression withered that idea. "Heaven knows I would like to, for I don't want the throne. For years, since long before the king named me Regent, we've been talking around in circles in Council meetings, arguing who should and shouldn't be the next king, but never making a decision until today. It might take years before they would be willing to accept you as the lost princess, but even then they would still argue over what to do, for in the end, they would force you to marry the man they chose. Because without an heir, we would be back in the same mess where we started. Stuck behind the Wall, unable to bring in anything from outside the kingdom, with cellars full of fifty years' worth of berry wine that we cannot trade for what we need."

"Why?"

"Because men are stubborn, and they have never been ruled by a woman before. They squawk like chickens if I suggest even the slightest change."

Rosamond shook her head. "No, why this embargo on trade? Did Father insist upon it, or our neighbours? Queen Margareta spoke of war, but only in jest. I can't imagine she or King Erik…"

But Margareta had given her the diseased cloth. Cloth that had nearly cost Warin and Monika their lives. Could she have done so on purpose, to wipe out her people? She weighed the possibility thoughtfully.

No, Rosamond decided. The plague in her body had been a far more advanced stage of the disease than what she'd seen in Monika or Warin's blood. Yet she had been the last of all three of them to touch the cloth. She most certainly hadn't caught it from the cloth but from the dressmaker's girl, Melitta. That laid the blame far from Margareta, who knew nothing of the girl's illness. In fact, that meant all of this was....

"My fault," Rosamond whispered. "Whatever ails the kingdom now is my fault. I thought by isolating myself in that convent, dying away from everyone else, I could save it, but I've only made matters worse. If I had done what my mother and father asked me to, I would have brought home a husband and settled down to have as many children as the kingdom needed to ensure the succession. Instead, I went haring about the palace, looking for a dress. I did not want a throne, but I wanted a dress like Queen Margareta's gown. Even when I realised what trouble I'd brought home, I thought my death would make things right. And now I am awake, I shall mess things up for you even more. Perhaps Warin was right, and I am cursed."

"No. You could not have known this would

happen. No one could have predicted the Wall." Siward sounded soothing, but his words were unsettling.

"What wall?" Rosamond asked.

"The wall of brambles that marks our borders, closing us off from the world," Siward explained.

"The berry bushes? I know they're old, but they are hardly menacing enough to be called a wall. Why, they have marked our borders for centuries before my time, and may still for centuries more." Rosamond shook her head. "The world might have changed much in fifty years, but you can't tell me berry bushes have suddenly turned from six-foot shrubs into towering trees."

Siward nodded, his expression serious. "That is almost exactly what I am telling you. They have formed a hedge more than thirty feet high in places, easily ten feet thick, ringing the kingdom round so that none may enter, and none may leave. Except for birds, and air."

"So cut it," Rosamond suggested. "We are a nation of farmers, labourers, woodcutters. Surely there are enough axes in the kingdom to keep a few bushes from getting out of hand."

"They tried that. For years, every man has tried his hand at chopping through the Wall, but for every blow you strike, it grows back into the breach. If you try to climb it, it sends you back to the ground. I have had swords and axes plucked from my hands countless times, for at the start of every summer, it is my duty as Lord Protector to test the Wall for weaknesses. I have never found one." He stared at her. "That is what I was doing when I found you."

Rosamond shook her head. "It must be magic, but who could put so much magic into miles and miles of bushes? To make plants behave so unnaturally, a witch would have to be constantly manning the Wall, pouring her power into it to keep it from being broken. How long has the Wall stood in its current state?"

Siward's gaze fixed on her. "Since the princess was lost."

Rosamond didn't miss the accusation in his tone. "You think this is my doing? That I would imprison my own kingdom, which I would have died to protect?"

"You're the witch, or so you say. You tell me."

Rosamond's hands clenched at her sides. "Show me this Wall."

Twenty Eight

It was several days' ride to the nearest section of Wall, but Rosamond did not complain once. She still appeared pale, but she had regained so much of her strength since their first ride together that she seemed like a different woman to the frail creature Siward had carried to his home only weeks before.

Knowing she was perhaps a princess did not change his opinion of her at all. If anything, it made him want her more. If he had to be king, though blood and birth had ill prepared him for such a role, better that he ascend the throne with her at his side. Her father had often said how he'd raised his daughter to rule, or he would never have sent her as an ambassador at such a young age.

If she'd been raised so differently to other girls, no wonder she held his interest so tenaciously. No other woman had ever invaded his thoughts quite so successfully. Even though she remained tucked firmly into her own bedroll on the opposite side of the fire, every night she stole into his dreams and reminded him of their first night together. If that was what it was like to bed a princess, he had no desire for any other woman.

No, that was not entirely true. What would it be like to bed her when she was queen?

Rosamond most certainly owned him, body and mind, even if she didn't know it yet, but she did not completely possess his heart. Not yet. Though he could feel her fingers closing around it...

What did it matter? They had shared one night together, when she'd mistaken him for another man. Now she knew the truth, he would never touch her again.

On the morrow, he brought her to where the Wall blocked the road.

She dismounted from her palfrey – she'd turned up her royal nose at the jennet Siward's groom had tried to give her, to Siward's amusement – and strode right up to the hedge. Like so many men before her, at first all she did was reach out to touch it, to confirm that what her eyes were seeing was true.

Then...she demonstrated how different she was. Closing her eyes, Rosamond pushed her sleeves up and thrust both hands elbow deep into the brambles.

Siward stepped forward to stop her. "Don't, you'll scratch yourself!"

Too late. A thin trickle of blood travelled down her arm before dripping to the ground. She didn't even seem to feel it.

"It's protecting us," she said slowly. "Keeping us from harm."

"How is keeping a kingdom prisoner protecting us?" Siward scoffed.

"They are plants, not politicians. They keep things out to protect us. Because...I wished it." Rosamond blinked. "They did this for me."

No evil queen, no curse, just a princess the plants wanted to protect? Siward wasn't sure what to believe any more. Rosamond didn't seem mad, and then she made such extraordinary statements that no one in their right mind would believe.

"Can you tell them to stop?" Siward ventured.

Rosamond's brow wrinkled. "I could try, but why would I? These brambles have kept us far safer than any castle wall for decades."

"They also stop trade. New knowledge, new stories. We are a small kingdom, and there are things in foreign lands that I can only imagine, for I have not seen them because we are closed to trade. We need metals, goods, food from other climates, somewhere to sell fifty years' worth of berry wine..." If Siward never tasted the stuff again, it would be too soon. He'd heard of something called beer, a drink like ale but with a finer flavour, which he'd always wanted to taste.

"I can ask them to give me a tunnel through which the road could run, as it did when I last saw this spot."

Siward could scarcely believe it. "Could you bring down the Wall?"

Rosamond pulled her arms from the bush. Though blood still stained her skin, there didn't seem to be a scratch on her. "I could, but I will not. A tunnel for the road will be sufficient. One that we can close again, if it is necessary."

Even that would be a miracle. "Do it, then!"

She folded her arms across her chest. "I will. When I am queen, and not before."

Siward's heart sank. This was an argument he sensed he would not win. Inwardly, he applauded the princess and her late father, the king. He had trained his replacement well.

"You would hold your own kingdom to ransom, just for a crown?" he asked heavily.

Rosamond smiled sweetly. "It is my kingdom, and my crown. I've laid down my life for it once, and while I did not die, I still paid a heavy price. If your Council does not want me, then they are fools who don't deserve me, or my powers. I will not touch the Wall until the kingdom is mine."

"You expect me and the rest of the Council to believe not only that you are their lost princess, miraculously alive and not aged a day after all these years, but that you alone can shift an impenetrable Wall that whole armies could not conquer?" Siward wasn't even sure he believed it.

She bit her lip. "Yes." She lifted her hand, tracing a lazy curve in the air. "You see?" Rosamond stared at the Wall with a slight smile on her lips.

Siward forced himself to turn around, both dreading and hoping for what he might see.

Branches twisted and moved, shaping a hole that grew larger as he watched it. The hole ended on the road, arcing up in an arch more than high enough for a mounted man to ride inside. Nay, not inside – through, he realised, as a shaft of sunlight shot through the tunnel from the other side.

Siward fell to his knees. "My God."

"No," Rosamond said sharply. "Your queen." And, with another wave of her hand, the tunnel closed as if it had never been.

Twenty-Nine

Siward said very little for the rest of that day, and most of the next. It was not until after dinner on the second night away from the Wall that he finally broke the silence between them.

"There is only one way you will be queen."

Rosamond sipped from her cup of wine. "Go on."

Siward hesitated. "You won't like it."

She stared at him across the fire, wishing she could read his thoughts. "I will not condone violence. The King's Council were appointed by my father, which meant he trusted their judgement, or at least their loyalty. I will not have them killed."

Siward looked stunned. "I had not considered that possibility."

Rosamond rose. "Then consider it now. I will not rule a kingdom by fear."

"But you would hold it to ransom with the Wall."

She waved his accusation away. "That is not the same. The Wall is not a threat. I am certain most people regard it as a simple fact of life. If it were to disappear overnight, or open with no explanation, then you will see fear. But if a rumour were to spread that the Wall appeared when the princess was lost, but it will open when she returns, and then you announce my miraculous return...the people will accept me, and the change."

Siward shook his head. "But not the Council. You will waste years arguing with them, and even then, they might not believe you. You might never regain the throne."

Rosamond stamped her foot in frustration. "No matter how stubborn they are, I will not let you kill them!"

Siward laughed softly. "Stubborn as they are, the Council are worth more to me alive. They at least had the good sense to make me king."

She glared at him. "So you're saying I should fight them, for however long it takes, while you steal my throne? I do not think so."

"I cannot steal what is freely given," he said. "And no matter what you do, I shall be king. You won't change their minds before my coronation, and afterwards...they will have their king. What will they want with a girl who claims to be a princess from a prior dynasty? They won't want to give you a crown, or a throne. No, they'll fight to wed you and bed you. Them, and their sons. For it is your blood they'll want, and the heirs they can beget on you. For if I fail, or die without an heir, they will have plenty of children with the right blood to plant in my place. They will never give their throne to a woman they consider little better than a brood mare."

"I am no one's bed toy. I was born to rule," Rosamond hissed.

Siward folded his arms across his chest. "There is a way. A way that will see you crowned queen before Midsummer."

"Tell me, and I shall do it."

Siward looked like he was holding back laughter. "Marry me."

Thirty

Rosamond looked like she wanted to leap over the fire and plant her fist in his face, Siward decided. But her court manners were too ingrained for her to do anything so uncouth.

"So that I can be your bed toy instead?" she demanded.

In his dreams. "If you wish, or I could be yours." Hastily, he continued, "At least consider it. Not a single man on the Council would question your right to be queen if you are my wife. Save your strength for what is truly important, instead of arguing with stubborn old men. If you care about your people and freeing the kingdom from the Wall so we can rejoin the outside world again, help me. Stand at my side so we can both lead our people into the future."

She looked thoughtful. "Why?"

Because he'd never met a woman he desired more, for both her body and her mind. From the moment he first saw her, he'd wanted her in his throne room. Now, he needed her. "Because you alone can save my kingdom, which makes you the perfect queen."

She slumped. "So you propose a marriage of convenience, then?"

If that was how she felt, then he would accept that she could never love him as she'd loved his grandfather. Siward wished he didn't feel so jealous of a dead man. "That is usually what happens when people pair for politics. Of course, the marriage must be real for appearances' sake."

Rosamond frowned. "What do you mean?"

"The Council will still expect us to produce an heir. They'd be happier with half a dozen, but one would be enough to start with."

If anything, her frown deepened.

He hastened to add, "I promise that every time you share my bed, I will endeavour to ensure you enjoy it just as much as you did our first night together." Siward swallowed. "Even if I have to fill the bed with flowers."

To his surprise, Rosamond laughed. "You would do that for me?"

Siward wasn't sure how to answer. Would she think him weak if he told the truth? Time to find out, he supposed, when no one but she would hear him.

"On that first night, when I first saw you, I thought I had died and heaven had given me a goddess for my own, like the heroes of old. I forgot everything of my life, my responsibilities, for my heart and my mind were full of nothing but you and how best to please you." Siward swallowed, then continued, "You have not left my thoughts for a moment since. Every day and every night, I think only of you. I would give you my whole kingdom in exchange for one more night of bliss with you."

She stared at him for a long time. He hoped she was considering his offer, instead of searching for the most diplomatic way to refuse him.

Then, almost as if she was unaware of what her hands were doing, Rosamond unlaced her gown and let it slide to the ground. Her shift soon followed, so that she stood naked in the firelight. "We have an accord," she said softly, her green eyes burning with desire.

Siward had to force himself to look away. "Good. On our wedding night, when we consummate our marriage, I shall claim my price."

"You drive a hard bargain, Lord Siward. But I accept."

Hard? She had no idea.

Finally, he heard the rustle of cloth as she covered herself, and Siward breathed again. He wasn't sure how he'd manage to wait the weeks until they were wed before he touched her again. But if she only allowed him one night…it would be worth the wait, he promised himself.

In the meantime, at least he had his dreams.

Thirty-One

On their return, Rosamond was caught up in such a whirlwind of activity she barely had time to think, let alone speak to Siward. She needed new gowns for her wedding and her coronation, plus more to wear to court afterwards, and at least a dozen new shifts and veils. Particularly as her newly rounded belly had started to show if her bodice was laced too tight.

What made matters worse was the first two gowns the dressmaker produced were made of scratchy, suffocating wool. And what in blazes had possessed her to make them blue?

"I asked for pink or green silk, not blue wool," Rosamond snapped at the woman. "I can't wear this in court, let alone at a coronation."

The woman dropped a deep curtsey. "I am sorry, mistress, but there is no silk to be had anywhere in the kingdom. Even if we did have some, we have no dye to make it the colours you desire. I have linen and wool, mistress, which I can make white and blue. Unless you can bring down the Wall so that traders can come in, this is all I can do."

All the more reason to get the formalities over with so she could fulfil her promise and poke a hole in the hedge. Unwilling to torment the poor dressmaker any further, Rosamond sent her to work on her new shifts instead. White linen, the woman assured her, would not be a problem.

When her coronation day arrived, Agnna laced her carefully into the same silk dress Rosamond had worn to Margareta's coronation, so many years ago. Mere months for Rosamond, of course, as she had slept through the intervening years, but so much had happened since that day. Rosamond prayed she could emulate Margareta's queenly demeanour today through all the layers of clothing and ceremony.

Once she made it through the day, she'd have the whole night to spend naked with Siward, Rosamond promised herself. True to his word, he had not touched her since she accepted his marriage proposal, and the longer she waited, the stronger her desire for him grew. Not that she would tell him so, of course. The man who usurped her throne could not be allowed to hold any power over her.

Like Margareta, she wore her hair uncovered, crowned in the same roses, though they were tinted a pale pink to match her dress. This time, it had taken barely a thought to make the flowers change colour, and not a whisper of dizziness. While she'd dreamed away fifty years, Rosamond's power had grown immeasurably. Though the Wall was miles away, all she had to do was touch another plant, and she could speak to them all, every tree and bush in the kingdom. The Wall itself felt like an army of soldiers, standing in formation, awaiting her orders. Tomorrow, she promised them.

Tomorrow, she would be queen.

Her palfrey stood ready outside, though Siward had left early to deal with important business in the palace, or so Agnna had said, so Rosamond rode alone to the city square, the open space between the castle and the cathedral. Today, it was far from empty. A huge bonfire stood in the centre, waiting to be lit, with a life-sized wicker figure tied to a pole at the top. Smaller bonfires dotted the square, and people milled around, chatting and buying food from the vendors who had set up their barrows on the edge of the space. Rosamond's stomach churned at the thought of food – she had no appetite today. Something felt wrong, but she could not identify what. Hooded and covered by her cloak, Rosamond urged her skittish mount through the crowd until she reached the refuge offered by the castle bailey.

There she found Siward, dressed in blue wool that still managed to look regal on him. When traders came to town, she would insist on buying him silks and velvets, as befit a king. For a moment, she forgot he was a usurper, and indulged her fantasies. He should have tunics tailored to show off his physique, widening at his broad shoulders as they narrowed to his taut belly. Cloaks of fur and velvet which would keep him warm even if he rode through the kingdom in the dead of winter. She would have new gowns that fitted her new curves perfectly, so that his eyes were drawn to her every moment she was in the room, banishing all other thoughts from his head. She would rule, not him, as it should be.

Rosamond dismounted and was assailed by a small feminine army, intent on brushing the travel dust from her clothes and making her look as perfect as a princess should on her wedding day. She knew none of them, but she thanked them graciously and swore to learn their names before the week was out.

They scuttled out of the way and Rosamond glanced up to see what had startled them.

Siward stood before her, looking more nervous than she felt. "It is time," he said, extending his arm.

Ah, yes. In the absence of her father, Rosamond was a ward of the crown, which meant the only man qualified to hand her over to her husband was the king-to-be. Some bright spark in charge of protocol had decided that meant she would enter the cathedral with Siward. They would kneel together and say their wedding vows, before they were crowned king and queen. Then they would walk arm in arm through the crowd to the castle, where they would change into rich clothes as befit the new royals, and a feast would be held in the great hall for all the noblemen and women of the kingdom.

Later that night, after the feast, Siward would carry her to the king's bedchamber and make the whole dull day worth it.

To Rosamond's surprise, it all proceeded as planned. Yes, she had stumbled over a broken tile in the cathedral on the way to the altar, and when Siward knelt on her skirt, he'd nearly torn the fragile fabric, but all his grandmother's threats came to naught when they spoke the vows that made them husband and wife. The priest raised his voice to proclaim their union to the assembled crowd, and a smattering of applause swept through the cathedral. Rosamond glanced over her shoulder. It looked like half the kingdom had tried to squeeze inside the vaulted building, and it sounded like the other half were waiting outside to congratulate the new king and queen.

Which brought them to the ceremony she'd anticipated most.

The priest who'd performed the wedding disappeared, to be replaced by a bishop who adored the sound of his own voice, or so it seemed to Rosamond. He sang, said prayers, and lectured them at length in a language Rosamond vaguely remembered from her childhood, but barely understood now.

Finally, an acolyte stepped forward with an ornate chest that Rosamond recognised, for it held the king's and queen's crowns. The bishop took the king's crown and loudly presented it to the four corners of the earth. Then, he lifted it high above Siward's head and called on the uncrowned king to make his vows of sovereignty.

Siward's voice rolled from his lips like velvet, caressing her ears and her heart as he promised to rule, protect, uphold and all the other things a good king did, casting a spell of his own over the crowd without any magic at all. Even Rosamond believed him. Siward would do all that he had promised, not because this was his kingdom, but because he was their king. The highest in the land, and yet their lowliest servant. She blinked back tears. He truly deserved the throne.

The bishop fussed around him, anointing him with oil and wrapping a fur cloak around his shoulders before droning through another prayer. After this interminable monologue finished, Siward was permitted to rise and take his place at a specially prepared throne on the dais. Then, it would be Rosamond's turn to receive the bishop's attentions.

The bishop reached into the ornate chest a second time.

"We're under attack!" a frenzied male voice shouted, before running feet pounded on the cathedral tiles. "The Wall has doubled in size, and now it is marching inward. It means to wipe us out!"

A man in torn clothing fell to his knees beside Rosamond. He smelled like he had not bathed in weeks. "The Wall, the Wall!" With a wink at Rosamond, the man collapsed in what appeared to be a dead faint.

Even amid the man's appalling stench, she smelled a rat, but in the panic that erupted, he was borne away from her before she could lay a healing hand on him.

She heard Siward and others shouting commands, but she ignored them all and made her way outside to the square. She scanned the space for something green, and found a rose vine that had climbed its way up the castle's outer wall. She grasped it and sent her thoughts winging across the kingdom to the Wall.

Which still waited, obedient to her command. Unmoving. Unchanged. The same size as the day she first touched it. And definitely not attacking anyone.

Whoever the smelly man was, he was a liar, sent to disrupt the coronation. She had to find Siward, to tell him the truth, so they could complete the ceremony. Now, more than ever, she needed to be queen.

Thirty-Two

When people exploded into panic all over the cathedral, Siward prayed for calm. He shrugged off the royal robe and set his crown on the throne he had occupied for barely a moment. What were they but empty symbols, anyway? More important was his promise to protect his people from all their enemies. Even that cursed plant.

Striding through the milling crowd, he shouted for a groom to saddle his horse, and pack provisions for a journey to the border.

Lord Vamos caught his arm. "The Council will

keep the peace until your return."

Siward thanked him, relieved. The Council might not be good at making decisions or agreeing to change, but they excelled at keeping the populace calm. Within moments, Lord Vamos had found the other Council members and led them purposefully toward the castle, like a mother duck with her brood.

His grandmother appeared from nowhere, clinging to him like a babe to its mother. "You will protect us, won't you? You'll turn the Wall back?"

Siward gently pried her off him. "Yes, Grandmother. I will ride immediately and do whatever I must to keep the kingdom safe." He glimpsed Rosamond on the other side of the square, looking lost beside a vine-covered wall. "While I am gone, take care of my wife. See her safely into the castle to await my return."

Lady Schutz followed his gaze, and she nodded. "I will see to her."

"Thank you." He thought for a moment. "What happened to Fodor? I would like to hear more of what he saw of the Wall."

Lady Schutz hung her head. "The poor boy rode day and night to get here to warn us, and it nearly killed him. He is resting, but I'm told it will be some time before he wakes. Time you can ill afford, if the Wall is advancing."

Siward nodded. She was right. Pausing only to ascertain that his saddlebags were full, Siward swung up into the saddle and set off at a gallop for the city gates.

Thirty-Three

Rosamond scanned the crowd, looking for Siward, but by the time she spotted him, he was already mounted and riding away. She screamed for him to come back, but he never heard her. He just kept on going. She slumped against the wall, defeated. Curling her fingers around the vine at her side, she whispered, "Bring him back to me safe, and keep him from harm."

Across the kingdom, a million leaves rustled in their promise to obey her command.

"There she is! The king's whore." Two men seized her arms, and when she struggled, a third grabbed her around the knees, too, lifting her off the ground and out of reach of the obedient vine. Between them, they dragged her to the foot of the cathedral steps.

"Is this the one, Lord Fodor?" the man on her left asked. He was the one who had called her a whore.

"That's the one," the smelly man said. "She's a whore and a witch, as the whole town of Hatar can attest. They saw her communing with the Wall. She danced naked before it, took her pleasure from its branches, before sacrificing the king's own hunting hawk to the devil and painting her wanton body with its blood. Then, still bathed in blood, she seduced the king by his own campfire, and bespelled him, so he would take her as his queen. She is a witch – the evil witch who cursed us with the Wall in the first place!"

Rosamond's mouth hung open in shock. Where had Fodor come up with these lies? It was almost as though he had followed her and Siward to the Wall, and sprinkled the story with the products of his own sordid imagination.

"She's been building an army in the Lord Protector's gardens, too! Tiny berry bushes, grown so huge they could consume a man, they would!" Draga piped up. "She's a witch, all right. Enchanted our poor king, she has!"

Siward's grandmother appeared at the top of the steps. "My poor grandson will not hear of her being tried for her crimes, for she has bewitched him. But now that he is gone, we shall see justice served. You all accuse her of witchcraft, casting evil spells against the kingdom and the king himself. That is treason. Is there anyone who can speak in her defence?" The hateful old woman scanned the crowd. "What, she has no champion? Or is it that there is no one who knows her, for she has travelled from outside the kingdom by magical means, to conquer us from within like the traitor she is!"

Loud cheering greeted this statement. Not just from the men Rosamond could see who restrained her, but from the hundreds, perhaps thousands of people standing behind her.

The old woman had incited a mob, and Rosamond knew there was no place for reason or sense in a mob. Fear's fingers closed around her heart.

Only Siward could stop this.

BRING HIM BACK! she screamed in her head, praying that the plants heard her, though she touched none.

"What say you to the charges, witch?" the crone demanded.

"I am your queen, and you will put me down. When the king hears of this, he will show no mercy." The last part was pure bluff, and Rosamond suspected the crone knew it. The men on either side of her loosened their grip, though, and the third let go of her legs entirely. This gave Rosamond the freedom to stand tall as she finished with, "If you cease telling your lies to my people, I shall see to it that you will not want for food or drink while you are in the dungeons. Perhaps I shall speak to the king, and you will not be executed."

Fodor spoke for them all, it seemed, when he strode forward, stopping so that his foul-smelling face was mere inches from Rosamond's. "Shut up, whore." His meaty fist crashed into the side of her head, sending her to the ground, where the paving stones stole her senses and the darkness gave her a reprieve from pain.

Thirty-Four

As he rode, Siward's head began to clear so he could think. The fastest way to the Wall was to change horses at the first town, and the next, and the next, resting only long enough to ensure he would not fall out of the saddle. He estimated he could make it to the Wall in a little over three days. It would still be another three days back to the city so that he and Rosamond could decide what to do about a Wall that wanted to attack, but he needed to gather intelligence before a strategy could be formed.

Rosamond knew more about plants and the Wall

than he did. Perhaps he should have brought her.

Siward considered this for a moment, then dismissed the idea. Her knowledge should be protected by castle walls and guards, not risked against an enemy none of them understood. If the Wall hurt her...

What could any of them do against the Wall?

Rosamond said it wanted to protect them. The Wall had healed her scratches – he'd seen it. He hadn't imagined the blood, nor the smooth skin she'd showed him afterward.

Why, after fifty years of doing nothing, would it attack now?

She could ask it. Rosamond said she could speak to plants, and in their own way, they responded to her. Protected her. Obeyed her wishes.

What if it only existed to protect her, and not the kingdom at all? What if waking her and taking her to the capital had summoned the Wall to protect her new home instead?

Rosamond would know. If it was necessary, she would take down the whole Wall, now he had fulfilled his part of the bargain and she was queen.

Siward reined in his horse, horrified as realisation struck him. She was not yet queen. Fodor, a rabid dog who had never left the city in his life, had interrupted her coronation before the bishop could complete the ritual.

What did Fodor have to gain out of this? The man never did anything unless it fed his own selfish desires.

His sister, the Lady Jolanka, who his grandmother had promised would be queen.

Who couldn't be queen while Rosamond reigned.

The Wall was right. Rosamond was in danger, and he was sworn to love and protect her.

Time to make good on that oath.

Siward swung his horse around, headed back the way they'd come. He made it a hundred yards before a tree branch plucked him out of the saddle. He hung in the air for a moment, clawing for a handhold, but he caught nothing, so he tumbled into the river that ran beside the road.

He came up spluttering and furious. "What was that for?" he shouted at the offending tree branch. "I'm trying to get home to help her!"

Every tree in the forest shook its leaves as though blown in a mighty storm. With one voice that sounded like an echo of Rosamond, they shrieked, "Bring him home!"

Thirty-Five

Rosamond's head ached. In truth, everything hurt, but her head was the worst. Her arms, from her wrists right up to her shoulders, burned, and so did her calves. Someone doused her in liquid and she spluttered, jerking awake.

She could see the whole city square from up here, for she was level with the cathedral's arched windows, and only a little lower than the castle battlements. That did not bode well, for the only thing high enough to give her such a vantage point was the Midsummer Eve bonfire with the wicker figure tied to the top.

Rosamond twisted her head, trying to see if she had guessed right. Indeed she had. She was tied to the effigy, and if she didn't do something, she would burn with it.

From the plague to this. No kingdom deserved to have a princess lay down her life twice for it.

"The witch is awake!" the smelly man shouted.

Fortunately, she could not smell him up here.

"You will rot in my dungeon," Rosamond called back.

"You have no power here, traitor!" the old woman shrieked.

It took Rosamond some time to work out where the old woman was. She stood atop the battlements, half hidden by the roses that had climbed the wall in their quest for sun. They would receive no warmth from Siward's grandmother.

"You are a witch, and a traitor. You seek to rule a kingdom that is not yours!" the woman announced.

Shouts of "Witch!" and "Traitor!" rose from the crowd that filled the square, all of them faceless now in the darkness. A faceless mob had no conscience, either.

"I seek to rule my rightful kingdom!" Rosamond shouted back. "I am Crown Princess Rosamond, daughter of King Almos and Queen Maria. His Majesty King Siward woke me from my enchanted sleep and brought me here so that I might rule by his side. This kingdom is mine, by right of blood and birth!"

The old woman hesitated, but she recovered quickly. "Imposter! I saw the princess's body with my own eyes, buried beneath the roses in a convent outside Hatar. She died fifty years ago, and you cannot be she!"

No. It was not possible. No one had entered that convent until the day Siward woke her. When Warin and Monika left, she had told the roses to enclose it completely.

That made the old woman…

"Monika!" Rosamond cried. All the people she had known in life had died, except for one – her loyal maid. "Monika, you of all people should recognise me. You were there when Queen Margareta gave me her crown!"

"Liar!" Monika shrieked. "You cannot be the princess, even if you look like she did the day she died. It is a trick of some sort, a spell only an evil witch could cast. And if you are not the princess, then you are the evil queen, who caused this kingdom so much grief. You killed our princess, cursed our land…and almost corrupted our king, but no longer! Tonight, you shall die, burned in the Midsummer bonfires like the devil-worshippers do to their own!"

Desperately, Rosamond tried to tell the vine on the wall to wrap around Monika's feet, to drag her out of sight so she would stop. Stop accusing her. Stop fighting her. Just...stop.

"Light the witch's pyre!" Fodor roared, thrusting his torch deep into the branches.

Stop them! Rosamond screamed in her head. Put out the fire. Don't let me burn.

As smoke rose up, obscuring her vision, she wrapped her hands around the pole behind her. It was green wood, still full of sap. She directed her thoughts into the dying sapling, urging it and all the wood around it to grow, to break the ropes tying her and help her down to the square.

It was no use. No tree could grow fast enough to save her, for all around the base of the pyre, a score of torches dipped to light the Midsummer blaze.

Thirty-Six

Siward rode up to the castle gates, sore, weary and soaked from his dip in the river. In the square, the townspeople were lighting bonfires for St John's Eve, as they did every year. He could even see the wicker man on one, a tradition that had its murky origins deep in the past. Something to do with fertility, was all he could remember. Perhaps that's why it looked so much like a woman, her skirts billowing in the rising smoke.

The bonfire caught, illuminating the figure, who was struggling to free herself from her bonds. Not wicker. A real, live woman.

"Stop them," the leaves on the trees whispered. "Don't let me burn."

Rosamond.

Siward slid from his horse, and shoved his way through the crowd. The flames leaped high above his head, but they had not touched her yet. If he could climb the woodpile and reach her in time, he could save her. A man stumbled into him, grabbing him by the shoulders. "Help me!" the man begged, as something dark trickled from his lips. He collapsed at Siward's feet, nearly tripping him, but Siward only leaped over the man and ran on.

Rosamond was the only one who mattered. The only one who could save his kingdom. Her kingdom. All this belonged to her.

Siward put on a burst of speed. Just before he reached the flames, he leaped, clawing for a handhold. The already smouldering branches burned his hands, but he hardly felt the pain. It would be nothing compared to the heart-wrenching agony of losing Rosamond.

Slipping twice, but climbing ever higher, he reached the top of the pyre. She had stopped struggling now and hung limp and lifeless from the stake they'd tied her to. Whoever had done this would pay with their lives, he swore.

But first, he had to save her. To cut her free and

climb down carrying her would take too long. Siward took a deep breath, then charged up to Rosamond, throwing all his weight against the post that held her fast. No, not a post, he realised as leaves showered down on him, but a fair-sized tree. An ominous crack sounded, but the tree did not break. He retreated a few steps further, to the edge of the flames, and charged again.

This time, his aim was true. The tree tilted and tipped, and Siward barely had a moment to wrap his arms around Rosamond to cushion her fall before all three of them tumbled down the side of the lit bonfire to the square below.

Thirty-Seven

"Siward?" Rosamond croaked, then coughed. Too much smoke. "Are you all right?"

His arm stuck out at an unnatural angle, and she could feel the pain rolling off him in waves. Broken ribs, and more besides, she guessed. Much like herself. The soot-smeared man groaned.

Rosamond squirmed around until she could see his face. Yes, he was her husband. His face looked merely smoke-blackened, and his wet, woollen clothes had protected the rest of him from the fire, but his hands…oh, his poor hands. So badly burned there was barely any skin left.

Their tumble had loosened her bonds, so she managed to get one hand free, then the other. Her feet could wait. She took Siward's bleeding, blackened hands in hers and kissed them, wishing with all her might that she had the energy to heal him. But all her magic had gone into the sapling that now lay on the paving, sprouting leaves and roots like it wished to start a forest in that very spot.

Still, she would do what she could. She seized a handful of leaves from the sapling's crown in one hand and lay her free hand over both of his. Closing her eyes, Rosamond drew every bit of power she could from the tree and poured it into Siward. She might not be their queen, but she would give her people back their king.

He let out a wordless cry and arched his back before another cry escaped, louder this time. Then…"Rosamond?" he said.

"I am here, my king," she replied. Even in her own ears, her voice sounded breathy and weak. "Healing you as best I can. It was…the least I could do. You saved my life."

"But if you heal me, who will heal you?" Siward asked.

No one.

The words seemed to echo around the square,

caught by the leaves of the trees and spun into the air.

Siward seized her shoulders. "Don't you dare go back to sleep on me. In fifty years, I'll be dead. Tell me how to heal you, Rosamond. You promised to be my queen, and we have yet to share a wedding night. I won't let you break your word."

Rosamond smiled. "The rose garden. In the castle. Take me there. If anything can heal me, they will."

He lifted her in his arms and followed her directions until they emerged in an unpaved courtyard. It looked nothing like the garden where she'd spent most of her youth, for fifty years of neglect had turned her regimented rose garden into a briar patch more overgrown than the convent where he'd first found her.

"Are you sure this is the place?" he asked doubtfully.

"I am certain. I can smell my roses, welcoming me home," she whispered. "Lay me down among them."

"But the thorns…"

"My roses will never hurt me. You have carried me far enough. I thank you for all you have done." It was a dismissal, but only a half-hearted one. For her heart longed for him to stay.

"I'm not leaving you. I've spent the night with you in a bed of roses before, and I intend to do it again."

Rosamond smiled. "As my king wishes." She

coughed again, then said, "I will sleep, and dream, as I work together with the plants to heal myself. If I do not wake with the dawn..."

He sounded fierce. "Then I give you fair warning. I shall kiss you until you do. Even if it takes hours."

Bliss, surely. "You are a brave man, my king. To lie alone and unprotected with a witch where her power is greatest."

Siward lay beside her on the briars, cushioned by roses, and took her in his arms. "I am not alone. I am with you."

Thirty-Eight

Midsummer's Day dawned, and it was glorious. King Siward held his bride in his arms, and though Rosamond's eyes were closed, they fluttered as if she was about to wake. Then she did, and her green eyes outshone the sun.

"Are you healed?" he asked softly.

She laughed. "Yes, and so are you. However did you get all those bruises?"

Siward thought hard. "I was attacked by a tree."

Amusement sparkled in her eyes. "You mean you weren't watching where you were going, and bumped into a tree?"

"Not this time. It whipped out a branch, grabbed me from the saddle, and threw me into the river. Then it screamed about how it had to bring me back. To you."

"A tree screamed? You must have hit your head."

Siward shook his head, which didn't hurt at all. "No. And not one tree. The whole forest screamed with the same voice. Your voice. Every tree ordering the others to 'bring him home'."

Rosamond wet her lips. "Truly?"

"Truly. And now I am home, I realise my queen has no crown."

Rosamond reached up for Queen Margareta's crown, which her captors had left on her head when they tied her to the stake, in mockery of her mother's gold crown, which she should have worn yesterday. Now she had neither, for the rose crown had disappeared. It was fitting.

"The people called me a witch. A traitor. Not a princess, and not their queen. They don't want me. They want you. Are loyal to you. I am…no one."

"Then we will change their minds. Slowly, at first, but some day soon, you will be more beloved as their queen than you ever were as their lost princess. I promise you." Siward rose from his bed among the roses, and held out his hand. "We have other promises to keep. First, we must go to the cathedral and finish what we started."

"But…"

"I promised you will be queen." The fervour in his eyes brooked no argument.

Rosamond accepted his assistance to rise, and, hand in hand, they walked out of the castle gates.

They did not notice, but if either had turned their heads to look, they would have seen two dead traitors, dangling from the battlements. No hand had yet touched them, for no one was willing to unwrap the choking rose vines from around Monika or Fodor's necks, or pry out the pine bough that had somehow impaled Fodor so that one end stuck out the bottom of his tunic, while the other jutted from the juncture of his neck and shoulder.

The square was empty but for ashes from the fires and a brittle circlet of dried roses that disintegrated in a puff of wind. Siward led Rosamond through the doors of the cathedral and shouted for the bishop.

Several minutes later, the bishop appeared, looking like he had dressed in a tearing hurry. He eyed the ragged, blackened pair before him. "What do you want?"

"For you to finish the coronation. My queen needs a crown."

When the bishop heard his king's voice, he fell to

his knees. "Forgive me, sire, I did not recognise you. Are you certain that you don't wish to wash before...?"

"I said crown her, now."

"Yyyyyes, sire."

In a gown of scorched silk, Crown Princess Rosamond knelt before the bishop. Like King Siward before her, she vowed to rule her kingdom fairly, protect its people and property, and uphold its laws for as long as she lived. She wept as she said the words, for they meant the end of all that had come before. The death of her parents, a goodbye to her childish dreams of freedom, and any desire to throw away duty, even for a day. But it was also a wondrous beginning, with Siward at her side.

Siward placed the royal cape around her shoulders, and the bishop set a crown on her head.

Queen Rosamond took her kingly husband's hand, and, both clad in radiant smiles that outshone the morning sun, they stepped out of the cathedral into a brand new day.

Thirty-Nine

Siward woke Rosamond with a kiss, as he had every morning for the last year since their wedding. "It is time," he said.

She smiled and stretched, still aching from the pleasure of last night's lovemaking. "So it is."

When they were both dressed, Siward opened the flap of their pavilion and led her out into the temporary village of tents that had sprung up beside the Wall.

The road ended where the hedge began, as it had for as long as anyone could remember, except

Rosamond. But now it was time to make new memories, which was why half the kingdom had come to see the spectacle. For today, their beloved queen would open the door to the outside world.

Letting go of Siward's arm, Rosamond approached the Wall. She traced a small circle on the hedge, spiralling outward until she had to use her whole arm to span the radius of her circle.

Gasps and murmurs arose from the crowd as Rosamond's magic began to make itself visible. A hole appeared in the Wall, big enough to insert a finger, but no more. The hole seemed to spin, widening as it went, until it could fit first a child's, then a man's hand. Yet still it grew, branches unfolding and undulating until they formed a perfect arch for the sun to shine through from the far side of the Wall for the first time in fifty-one years.

Cheering and clapping erupted, but the show was not over yet. Rosamond took Siward's arm once more, and together the king and queen strode through the arch across the border. Then in view of everyone, they turned to each other and kissed.

On the inside of the Wall, a baby started wailing.

The king and queen returned home.

"The queen commands the Wall, to be our defence when we are in need, but she will open the door for all those who wish to pass through. For it might have been cursed by an evil queen, but she is no match for the power of Queen Rosamond the Fair!"

The wailing baby did not care for King Siward's speech, and the loud cheering from the crowd only made him scream louder still.

Rosamond sighed. "Lady Jolanka, bring him here." She held out her arms, but Siward plucked the baby from her companion's arms first.

"What's wrong, Helios?" Siward asked his infant son.

"Selene hit him, or pinched him, I am certain of it," Jolanka said, sounding quite proud of the girl as she thrust a beaming baby Selene at her mother. "You'd better name her heir to the throne and not him. She's the fighter, and the elder, too."

"We shall see," Rosamond said. "The king and I have many years yet, in which to live happily ever after. The tale of our twins…is yet to be told."

Author's Note

If you're looking for more fairy tale retellings…here's a
sneak peek from *Dance: Cinderella Retold*, the next book
in the series.

Bonus Sneak Peek of
Dance: Cinderella Retold

Mai rode at the head of an army, or at least she thought she did, until the city of Dean rose into view. What she saw made the troops at her back look like a troupe of travelling performers after a night of carousing. Tired, undisciplined and dirty. Mai barely noticed as the men were marched off to one of the fortified camps ringing the city around. She was too busy marvelling at the construction that had gone into besieging an entire city.

"You're to report to General Li," the messenger said, interrupting Mai's battle plans. "I'll take you to the command tent, and then I can return to the capital. Where things are civilised."

Mai followed him into the biggest stockade, which sat on a natural rise on the otherwise flat plain. The General's tent was actually a wooden hut, built on a mound of earth in the middle of camp, overlooking what appeared to be a training ground. The General himself was the only man in full armour, though he carried his helmet under his arm as he watched the troops training below.

No, not training. Sparring, Mai noticed with interest. She had not trained with an opponent since she left her father's household, and she was eager to learn to fight better against someone more skilled than she.

"This is the last one. Yeong Mao, Yeong Fu's son," the messenger announced, shoving Mai forward so that she almost overbalanced.

She righted herself before she fell at the General's feet. "My father sent me to learn the art of war, General," Mai said. "He has trained me well."

General Li snorted. "That's what they all say, right up until they turn and run in battle. Cowards. Right. Whatever-your-name-is, go join the other young noblemen down there. First, we'll see how well you can fight, and then give you something to do."

He turned to speak to one of his aides, effectively dismissing her.

The messenger seemed mesmerised by the group of young men the General had pointed to. "Good luck, Yeong Mao," he said softly.

Mai swallowed. "Thank you," she said. "I wish you a safe journey back to the capital."

She joined the circle of boys, who formed a ring around two combatants. The smaller of the two, a boy perhaps a year or two older than Mai and not much bigger, struggled to hold his wooden sword aloft, even as he gripped the hilt with both shaking hands. The other boy – no, a man, Mai decided, smacked his own wooden blade against it almost lazily, sending the smaller boy's sword flying across the circle to land at Mai's feet.

Mai reached down for the sword, which felt surprisingly light in her hand. Her father's wooden blades had a metal core, weighting them much like a proper sword, but this one was all wood. She looked up, intended to offer the practice blade back to the disarmed boy, but he now lay on his belly in the dirt, begging for mercy from the bigger boy whose blade merely touched the back of the downed boy's neck.

"Next," the victor drawled, letting his foe up.

The boy scrambled out of the circle as fast as his

feet could carry him.

The next challenger was built like an ox. He would have no trouble lifting the light sword, Mai thought, as he tossed it from hand to hand like it weighed nothing. Then the challenger adopted a bold stance, knees bent, facing the victor of the previous bout.

"Try that on someone your own size!" the challenger called.

The victor strode forward, his muscles bunching as he delivered his first thrust.

The challenger managed a clumsy block, but his movements were too slow. He might have the strength to fight, but he had had little practice with a sword, Mai decided. The victor delivered a series of slashing blows that his opponent barely managed to block in time, until one cut made it through, tearing through the fabric of the boy's tunic.

Mai glimpsed pale flesh for a moment before the boy dropped his blade, turned tail and ran out of the circle.

"The General will put him to good use, running messages in battle!" the victor said.

A few of the boys in the circle sniggered at this, but the laughter died quickly when they realised the man in the middle wasn't laughing. Instead, he pointed at those who had. "You, you and you. In that order. You're up next."

The boys ducked their heads in obedience, and the first one trudged across the dirt to meet his fate.

Without taking her eyes off the fight, Mai asked the boy beside her, "Who is he?"

"The Prince of Swords, Jun Yi," the boy whispered. "Best swordsman in the kingdom, or so he says. No one's managed to beat him yet. The General said if we can stay on our feet for a turn of the hourglass in the ring with him, we will be assigned to his camp, and will lead troops in battle. when we breach the city walls. The rest of us will go to different watchtowers to stand guard over the city."

Stand guard? There was no honour in guard duty. Leading troops into battle…if Mai wanted to earn honour for her family, and avoid being married off, then she must find a way to fight this Prince of Swords.

"How many have beaten the hourglass?" Mai asked.

The boy swallowed. "So far, none."

The Prince of Swords was a master swordsman indeed, then. An enemy she must know as well as she knew herself, for Mai to be victorious.

For the first time, she took a good look at the man, instead of his less skilled opponents. Jun Yi lowered his head and barrelled into a boy, knocking him into the dirt. Jun Yi was a big man, who used his size and strength to his advantage against smaller opponents like this one. He held his sword like a man who had trained for longer than Mai had, for it moved with a fluidity that spoke of experience and a good teacher. His sword truly was an extension of his arm – and a long arm, too. He used his bigger reach to attack his opponents before they had the chance to touch him, forcing them to defend against a fast flurry of blows that were designed to distract, not hit, until Jun Yi saw an opening and took it. Not to hurt or to kill – no, he knocked his opponent down. In battle, his enemy would be trampled or run through, Mai knew. She suspected Jun Yi did, too.

She watched him peel off his sweat-soaked tunic and use it to mop his face. Her belly sort of swirled a little, as if she was suddenly hungry for something. Strange. She'd eaten some of her travel rations only an hour ago. Why the sight of a man's muscled body made her feel hungry again, she had no idea. Yet as she stared, she realised he had an impressive collection of scars. Battle scars. Jun Yi was a veteran of many battles, if his back was any indication. He would definitely lead troops into battle on the assault on the city. Perhaps he already had – many times. Now Mai's hunger took a different turn – she hungered for his knowledge and experience, so that she might lead troops to victory, too.

"Any of you other ladies want to come and dance

with me?" Jun Yi asked, turning slowly on the spot so he could meet the eyes of every boy who dared raise his gaze from the dirt. "Or will you all be standing guard on the watchtowers like the others?"

Mai stepped forward. "I shall dance with you."

The tale continues in the next book in the series
Dance:
Cinderella Retold

About the Author

Demelza Carlton has always loved the ocean, but on her first snorkelling trip she found she was afraid of fish.

She has since swum with sea lions, sharks and sea cucumbers and stood on spray drenched cliffs over a seething sea as a seven-metre cyclonic swell surged in, shattering a shipwreck below.

Demelza now lives in Perth, Western Australia, the shark attack capital of the world.

The *Ocean's Gift* series was her first foray into fiction, followed by her suspense thriller *Nightmares* trilogy. She swears the *Mel Goes to Hell* series ambushed her on a crowded train and wouldn't leave her alone.

Want to know more? You can follow Demelza on Facebook, Twitter, YouTube or her website, Demelza Carlton's Place at:

www.demelzacarlton.com

Books by Demelza Carlton

Ocean's Gift series

Ocean's Gift (#1)

Ocean's Infiltrator (#2)

Ocean's Depths (#3)

Water and Fire

Turbulence and Triumph series

Ocean's Justice (#1)

Ocean's Trial (#2)

Ocean's Triumph (#3)

Ocean's Ride (#4)

Ocean's Cage (#5)

Ocean's Birth (#6)

How To Catch Crabs

Nightmares Trilogy

Nightmares of Caitlin Lockyer (#1)

Necessary Evil of Nathan Miller (#2)

Afterlife of Alana Miller (#3)

Mel Goes to Hell series

Welcome to Hell (#1)
See You in Hell (#2)
Mel Goes to Hell (#3)
To Hell and Back (#4)
The Holiday From Hell (#5)
All Hell Breaks Loose (#6)

Romance Island Resort series

Maid for the Rock Star (#1)
The Rock Star's Email Order Bride (#2)
The Rock Star's Virginity (#3)
The Rock Star and the Billionaire (#4)
The Rock Star Wants A Wife (#5)
The Rock Star's Wedding (#6)
Maid for the South Pole (#7)
Jailbird Bride (#8)

The Complex series

Halcyon

Romance a Medieval Fairytale series

Enchant: Beauty and the Beast Retold (#1)
Awaken: Sleeping Beauty Retold (#2)
Dance: Cinderella Retold (#3)

www.ingramcontent.com/pod-product-compliance
Lightning Source LLC
Chambersburg PA
CBHW070506120726
47910CB00003B/1134